THE BILLIONAIRE'S BEAUTY

FAIRY TALE BILLIONAIRES

AVA RYAN

1

GRIFFIN

"ABOUT FUCKING TIME, FOREST," I say.

I set my gin and tonic on the table and accept the thick envelope from my assistant, Bellamy Forest, when she arrives at my table. I'm enjoying celebratory drinks with my younger brother and business partner, Ryker, because we closed a big deal this afternoon. Our eldest brother, Damon, was also here, at least until he caught sight of some sultry redhead at another table a few minutes ago and took off for a closer look.

Bemelmans on the Upper East Side isn't exactly the place for conducting business, especially with both the pianist and the crowd in full swing, but I need to spend a good chunk of my weekend reviewing these documents before the closing on Monday. Sucks for me, but it's tough out here for a real estate mogul who wants to stay on top of his game. True, I could have arranged for a courier to deliver the documents, but Bellamy is my right-hand person. One of the very few trustworthy people I know. Has been since the second she walked into my life a year ago. And she might as well earn the big bucks I pay her to keep my trains running on time. Even if it is both her twenty-sixth birthday and a Friday night, as evidenced by the spiky heels and little black dress she seems to be wearing under her blue shawl.

"Guess I'll cancel that missing persons report I just phoned in," I add.

An asshole comment? Of course. But I'm an asshole. Ask anyone. Luckily, Bellamy's salary includes a hardship premium for dealing with me, and we've developed a system. I make a comment like that, she responds with a sarcastic little reminder of what a jackass I am, something like "Sorry, boss. Didn't realize there was traffic in Manhattan" and we keep it moving. I'm a busy guy. I don't have time to make friends. She understands that. That's why we get along so well professionally. We have our roles and we stick to them.

Which is why I'm surprised when she says the following:

"Sorry, boss. Cops put a boot on my magic carpet. It was double-parked. Are we done here? I'd love to enjoy my twenty-sixth birthday before my twenty-seventh rolls around. Unless you plan to ruin my entire night."

I'd just tossed the envelope onto the table and started to reach for my drink again, but now I freeze. Exchange startled looks with my brother just to make sure I really heard that edgy tone coming from *her* mouth. Glance up and take a good look at Bellamy for the first time, wondering if I've been imagining the way she's gotten under my skin in the last several days.

Bellamy is crisp. She is cool. She is eminently professional. The thing she is not? Challenging. The thing she does not do? Make me think about her as a person.

As a woman.

But no, there it is. The veiled *What are you going to do about it?* in her stiff posture, squared shoulders and glinting brown eyes.

And, I gotta tell you, I find it fascinating.

One other thing I should mention? Bellamy Forest is easy on the eyes.

Look, I'm a heterosexual guy. I'm into women. Into everything about women. All women are beautiful.

But Bellamy Forest is *beautiful.* About average height, she's a perfect figure eight, with plenty of boobs in front, tons of ass out back and a tiny waist in between. She's *fit*, with toned legs and shoulders.

I love a fit woman.

And let's talk about her face for a minute. Big brown eyes, like I said. Cute little nose. X-rated mouth. English rose complexion. The kind of long and sun-kissed wavy brown hair that belongs in some glossy magazine ad for a high-end salon.

I'm not going to lie. I noticed all that about Bellamy the second she walked into my office for her interview a year ago. I also noticed her summa cum laude degree from Barnard College, her full-time gig as a tutor that helped her finance said degree and her ambition to work her amazing ass off and save money for law school. I can control my baser impulses when necessary, and it was necessary if I wanted to hire the best candidate for the job. Not to mention the fact that I don't want to get sued for sexual harassment. So I put my dick on lockdown, my attraction to her on a shelf and hired her.

Things have worked out great. Until now.

Now? My attraction is off that shelf. It didn't ask for my permission to jump down. It just did. And my dick is starting to seriously resent the lockdown.

"Actually, we're *not* done." I stare her dead in the face, eager to see what she'll do next. Not a good idea, for which I partially blame this second gin and tonic. "I'm going to need you for a bit longer tonight. You might want to let your friends know you'll be late."

Confession: I went to the office kitchen earlier for a cup of coffee, during which time I overheard Bellamy discussing tonight's plans with another staffer that she's friendly with. Naturally, they hushed up when I walked into the room, but not before I heard mention of drinks, dinner, a club and some sexy guy everyone wants Bellamy to meet. Not that anyone asked my opinion, but I was fine with all of it. Until I heard about this sexy guy. The idea of Bellamy hooking up with some faceless sexy guy rubs me the wrong way.

Matter of fact, it rubs me so wrong that it wrecked most of my afternoon while I tried to convince myself that I'm not jealous.

This was an unexpected and unwelcome development. I can't figure out when things went sideways on me. Can't stop wishing I could get this runaway genie back in the bottle.

Don't get me wrong. Bellamy is a grown woman. I'm sure she's had sex since she joined my company's payroll. I never thought about it. Never cared. Until this afternoon, when the information about her personal life whacked me on the back of the head like a nail-studded two-by-four swung by Barry Bonds.

The bottom line? I don't like the idea of my Bellamy (not that she's *my* Bellamy, but you know what I mean) spending her birthday fucking some loser, and I'm not crying over the fact that I have the power to put the kibosh on those plans, at least temporarily.

I'm not crying at all.

She blinks. Reins in her frown with what looks like a significant amount of effort. "How late?"

"Hard to say," I say, shrugging. "Will that be a problem?"

To her credit, she manages a smile. A crooked smile, but still credible.

"Not at all," she says, glancing around just as a nearby couple get up and leave their table. "Why don't I just sit over there, since there's no room at this table? Damon. Ryker. Hope you two have a great night."

"Hope you get to enjoy what's left of your birthday, Bellamy," Ryker says.

"Don't let him give you too much shit, Bellamy," Damon tells her.

"Don't worry," she says, laughing. "I've got this."

With that, she turns to go while also unwrapping that blue shawl and giving me a spectacular and mouth-watering view of the body she normally keeps tucked inside her business attire. Tonight? It's poured into a little black dress with heavy emphasis on *little*. It's got no sleeves. No nothing other than a stretchy tube that bares a fair amount of cleavage before clinging to her hips and ass and trailing off well before it hits her knees. But before I can lament the fact that I can't see much of her legs, she takes another step, revealing a slit and a juicy stretch of thigh.

The sort of thigh a man wants wrapped around his waist when he's buried deep inside a gorgeous woman.

I'm not shitting you when I say that the sight of that glowing skin, shifting hair and insane figure is like a lightning strike to my entire existence.

My head commands me not to do anything stupid.

My dick commands me to fuck her as soon as possible. Something deep inside me—trapped somewhere between my chest and my gut—wonders what the *fuck* is happening to my world tonight.

My turmoil is intensified when she glances back over her shoulder and gives me just enough of a lingering look for me to wonder if she wants me to come hither.

Or maybe that's just my runaway hormones projecting things onto her.

Doesn't matter. I'm already on my feet, determined to follow her like a heat-seeking missile.

2

GRIFFIN

I'M SO focused on my knee-jerk need to follow Bellamy and explore my new attraction to her that the rest of the crowd—hell, universe—drops from view. Until Ryker clamps a heavy hand on my wrist and stops me. Much to my annoyance.

"What?" I snarl, yanking free and keeping one eye on Bellamy as she sits at the new table with her back to me. The last thing I want is for her to slip away when I'm not looking while I waste time with this clown.

My brother gapes up at me as though I've started sprouting toes for eyebrows. "I know that look. What's gotten into you?"

The urgency in his quiet voice pierces my haze of lust. I take a deep breath. Remind myself that I'm not a stallion on the scent of a mare in heat.

"Nothing," I say, checking my cuffs and smoothing my hair because my fidgety hands need something to do. "We done?"

"Listen. Don't do anything stupid. Bellamy's the best

assistant you've ever had. Not to mention the fact that we don't need to be sued for sexual harassment. So let it go. There are other fish in the sea."

"Have you seen a fish like *that* one lately?" I say without hesitation, in the clearest sign yet that I've lost my mind.

"Read my lips, lover boy." He gives me a hard and unblinking stare. "Don't. Do. It. Find another way to mess up your life that doesn't involve our company."

He's right, I decide, deflating as I realize the full extent of my idiocy. I hate him for it, but he's right. With a curt nod and a final glare lobbed in his direction, I head off to join Bellamy. She watches me sit with a pleasant smile, from all appearances blithely unaware of the bombshells she keeps detonating inside my head tonight.

"Everything okay?"

"Yep," I say, my mood now curdled like milk that's been left in the sun all day. So I can't have Bellamy. Can't stare at the enticing spot where her dress dips low in front, revealing her plump breasts. Even though it's *right* in front of my face. *Fine.* At least I can get a little work done before I let her go to resume her regularly scheduled birthday events. "Let's get started. I'm thinking we need to—"

"Hang on. You're not going to buy me a drink?"

"—get started on the— *What*?"

"A *drink*," she says, putting a hard emphasis on the K at the end. "It's the least you can do. Since you're ruining my birthday and all."

"I'm happy to get you a drink," I say, signaling for the server. "But I want the record to reflect that I gave you a birthday bonus this morning. That counts for something."

"It does count for something. It counts for this dress. And the shoes. Which I snuck out and got on my lunch break."

"Ah," I say, focusing all my energy on hoisting my gaze back up to her face every time it wants to dip lower. The effort is going to cause me to break out in a sweat in a moment. "Nice. What'll you have?"

"Champagne," she says as the server arrives at the table. "Order the good stuff."

"The good stuff?" I say on a choked laugh.

She shrugs those kissable shoulders. "It's my birthday. I should get some of what I want on my birthday. That's a rule."

I might be imagining things again, but I'd swear there's a silky note in her voice now. And a disquieting gleam of something in her steady gaze as she watches me across the table.

"Besides," she adds. "I'm worth it."

I can only imagine. If her performance in the bedroom is anything like her performance at the office, she's hella worth it.

I somehow manage to rip my attention away from her, focus on the server for two seconds and order a bottle. Their nicest bottle, by the way. When the man walks off, my curiosity reverts to Bellamy and gets the best of me.

There was a lot of subtext in what she just said. A follow-up question seems appropriate.

"*Some* of what you want?" I ask her.

She hesitates. I live and die in that hesitation.

"I'd be surprised if I got everything I wanted." She smiles, but it's rueful. Something about it causes an ache in my chest. "Probably only people like you get everything they want."

In the long pause that follows, I think about, how much I want to peel that dress off her, inch by inch. How much I want her scratches on my back and her tongue in my mouth. How much I want to hear my name on her lips when I make her come. And come and come and *come*.

"I don't get everything I want," I say flatly. "Take my word for it."

The server returns just then, preventing me from seeing Bellamy's unfiltered reaction to this information. He pops the cork and pours for us, then leaves us to our awkward silence. I wonder why Bellamy's face and presence, which are constantly by my side at the office, now feel so unusual and intriguing.

Is the rosy romantic lighting at Bemelmans that good? Does that expensive little black dress of hers contain a magical sprinkling of some potent sex potion I need to know about?

Or has my simmering attraction for her finally exceeded my ability to keep it under wraps?

"Anyway," I say gruffly, raising my glass and renewing my determination to behave like the professional I purport to be. No matter what signals I imagine she's shooting my way. "Here's to the upcoming year. Hope it's a great one. Cheers."

I give her glass a quick clink—

"Hang on," she says, pulling her glass back and frowning. "We have to make eye contact."

"Huh?"

"Otherwise, we each have bad sex for a year," she

says, her gaze direct and unwavering. Almost...*bold*. "It's a rule. I'm surprised you've never heard of it."

I blink and try to get my head on straight, because I swear there's a smolder deep in her eyes. That vague challenge is also back in her voice. For the life of me, I can't get a bead on what she thinks she's doing here. If she thinks I'm going to clink her again so she can have great sex with someone else, she'd better think again. And if she thinks I won't take her up on her challenge to fuck her if she keeps looking at me like that, I'm more than happy to take her back to my place and prove her wrong.

All that scrolls through my mind in that blink of my eye, quickly followed by an unwelcome voice of reason.

Don't do it, asshole.

"Cheers," I say, maintaining eye contact this time. I gulp back half of my champagne and set my glass down. Then I rub my hands over my face and try to get my brain back online enough to remember my scrolling to-do list.

"So I need you to, ah, book my flight to Tokyo for a week from Thursday through that Monday. That's first. Get the car and the, ah, driver lined up. All that. The usual. I liked that suite I stayed in the last time, so get that one again. Talk to them about making sure the cappuccino machine is there when I arrive. Also some of that sake I liked. Then we need to start looking at party planning for the event in the Hamptons. We're going to have a lot of high rollers there, so we want to make sure..."

I trail off when it dawns on me that she's not taking notes on her phone the way she always does.

"What's the problem?" I say, frowning. "You getting all this?"

"Absolutely." She downs all her champagne, then waves her glass at me for a refill. "I've done most of it already, anyway."

That's one of the reasons I keep Bellamy around. She's got a great memory and an uncanny ability to juggle all the plates I've got in the air at any one time.

"Great," I say, topping her off and then watching with vague unease as she kills it. "Have you got an alcohol problem I need to know about, Forest? Because we've got a shit-ton of work to do. I don't have time to send you off to rehab."

"Nope," she says tightly, stifling a burp as best she can. "No problems here. None whatsoever. Never. Been. Better."

"Well, that's good," I say. "What was I saying about the Hamptons? Oh, yeah. We need to—"

"Actually, I *do* have a problem." She nails me with a look that suggests I've been popping balloons beside sleeping babies. "Are you ever going to call me *Bellamy*? Which is my name? Or maybe Bella, like my friends do?"

"*Why?*" I say, recoiling because I can't think when I've heard a worse idea. I'm trying to maintain a professional distance between myself and Bellamy and keep frantically trying to throw bricks onto the wall between us. Calling her by her first name would be removing bricks from the wall. Plus, it wouldn't feel right to say, for example, *I want to fuck you, Forest*. On the other hand, *I want to fuck you, Bellamy* rolls right off the tongue. "You call me *boss*. I call you *Forest*. Why switch it up?"

"It's after hours. We're having drinks."

Exactly.

"I wouldn't want to cross any lines," I say, shaking my head.

"No." One corner of her luscious mouth pulls back into a crooked smile that perfectly matches the complete lack of humor in her eyes as she waves her empty glass at me again. "The one thing we'd never want to do is cross any lines. *Boss.*"

A beat or two passes while I try to figure out what the hell is going on here. Why I'm feeling this push–pull from her tonight.

"What's up, Forest?" Not the sort of question you should ask when you want to keep things professional, but I can't seem to help myself. "Because I'm getting the feeling you've got something on your mind. Something I'm missing."

Her expression softens until she looks almost wistful. I wait, inexplicably feeling as though a large slice of me is tied up in her answer.

"I doubt you'd understand. Boss."

I lean closer. "You could try me."

She opens her mouth. Hesitates.

"Probably a bad idea," she finally says with an unmistakable tinge of regret.

I feel a tiny stab of disappointment.

Not so tiny. More like a vertical slice through my chest, which is ridiculous.

But you can't control your feelings, which is one of the reasons I make it my policy never to feel them if possible. I give myself a swift mental kick in the ass and try to keep things in perspective here. I want Bellamy, sure, but I'm not dying without her. Maybe I imagined the chemistry between us tonight. Maybe I didn't.

Maybe she really does feel as attracted to me as I feel to her but has now decided not to act on it. The fine details don't really matter. Either way, me hooking up with Bellamy—who is still, by the way, my most valued employee, whether we're attracted to each other or not—is a no-go.

That's for the best. And I'm grateful one of us is smart enough to see that.

"Okay." I raise my brows as she evidently decides I'm moving too slow and refills her own glass this time, jamming the bottle back into the bucket with a little more force than necessary, and try to get back to business. "Where was I? Oh, I think I have a dentist appointment for that block when I'm in Tokyo, so make sure you kick that. Also, I feel like somebody's birthday is coming up...?"

"Your uncle's."

"Right," I say, snapping my fingers. "So we need to get him something. He liked that case of scotch you ordered him last year. Get that again."

"You got it, boss," she says dully.

"There's some light that came on in my car. Get that scheduled for an appointment."

"Which one?"

"I think it's the one for maintenance."

"Which *car*?"

"Oh. The Maybach."

"Got it. And what about your flowers for the week?"

"My...flowers?" I ask dumbly, stalling for time. This is the sort of discussion we have all the time. Yet tonight I feel intensely awkward, as though she's asked me about my masturbation preferences.

"Yes. Your flowers. Who will we be sending them to

this week? Brenda again? Allison? Someone new you'll meet later tonight? What are my marching orders? I like to give the florist a heads-up on orders as large as yours."

Another confession: I'm a flower sender. Have been for years, ever since I discovered that sending an ostentatious bouquet of flowers (which, while expensive, is cheaper than jewelry) tends to soften the blow of rejection out here in the dangerous world of dating. Not that I ever really *date*, but you know what I mean. One-night stand with a woman you never plan to see again? Send flowers. In a casual relationship with someone whose birthday you forgot? Send flowers. Looking forward to a special night with a woman you've never fucked before but hope to fuck tonight? Send flowers. Trying to untangle yourself from a fuck buddy who now thinks the relationship has growth potential? Send flowers. At any given moment, I tend to have a woman on the field, a woman warming up in the bullpen and a woman I've scouted but have yet to recruit to my team. The upshot? A lot of flower sending for Bellamy. Who no doubt thinks I'm a world-class player.

She's right.

I check my cuffs again, my cheeks and ears burning. I'd planned to hook up with a woman I met at the gym the other day named Candy (Cindy?). She gave me her number and told me to call her anytime, all but removing her panties on the spot and handing them to me as I cooled down on the treadmill.

But now? Candy/Cindy is the last person on my mind. And it suddenly seems crucial to up Bellamy's low opinion of me and my romantic exploits.

"No flowers this week."

"Great," she says crisply. "That's just cut my workload in half. Anything else? Because I'd like to go join my friends. But first, I've had a little bit of news I need to tell you about."

"Ah, yeah," I say, racking my brain to try to think of any other reason to keep her around and coming up short. "We're done. What's up?"

"I'm quitting."

3

GRIFFIN

WHY DO people always think it's a joke when they hear bad news? Either that, or they ask for a repeat of the bad news, as if they've suffered some instantaneous and catastrophic hearing loss that prevents them from hearing correctly. The brain's way of trying to un-hear what it doesn't want to be true, I guess.

Whatever it is, it's got me in a chokehold.

I cock my head, determined to try this again and hear it right this time.

"*What?*"

"I'm quitting," she says again.

I manage half a strangled laugh. "No, the fuck you're not."

"Well, okay," she says calmly. That's one of the most reliable and infuriating things about Bellamy. She's always calm. "That settles it, then."

"How are we doing over here?" the server asks brightly, reappearing at table side. "Can I get you —"

"*No,*" I bark, my attention irrevocably centered on Bellamy the Calm and only dimly aware of the man walking off again. This is between Bellamy and me. I need her, and she's kicking me to the curb like she doesn't have a care in the world. The rest of the world, including the pianist, who's over there plinking away on some Frank Sinatra tune, can fend for itself while I figure out why. "I'll give you a fifty percent raise. Now drop the nonsense."

She hesitates.

"Sorry, boss. I can't do that."

The B-word suddenly grates on my nerves in a way it never has before.

"I'll double your salary. And don't call me *boss*."

Her expression turns to stone right in front of my eyes.

"I have a good reason for quitting—"

"Doubtful."

"And I think I'll stick with *boss*. Since you just sat there and told me you didn't want to cross any lines."

"That was before you ripped the rug out from under me," I say, planting my elbows and hunkering over the table. "What the fuck is going on?"

She hitches up her chin. Beams with unmistakable pride.

"I heard from Berkeley Law. I'm off the waiting list. It's my dream school. My mother went there. Anyway, I start in August."

Rarely has anyone gone through such a sickening cycle of emotions. My anger evaporates. I feel enormous excitement for her because this is her dream come true and I know it. I feel proud of her accomplishment. I feel eager to see how big a bite she'll take out of the legal world. I feel concern because I know how much Berkeley costs versus how much I've been paying her, and those two numbers don't equal each other. I feel a strong urge to volunteer to pay for her entire legal education and bookmark that idea for later. I know how poignant this moment must be for her because her mother died a few years ago and isn't here to see her daughter fly.

Most of all? I feel flattened. Because soon Bellamy will be living three thousand miles away.

She really is leaving. There really is nothing I can do to stop her.

And I'm sure the sickening knot in my gut has nothing to do with her skills as my assistant.

I blow out a harsh breath. Rub my hands over my face. Drop my hands, face her like a man and try to approximate a selfless human being.

"That's amazing," I say, meaning it even if I can't quite force my lips into a smile. "Congratulations. The legal world is going to get a hell of a lawyer once you're all trained up. I know it."

"Thanks," she says, now beaming at me as though I've slipped the Hope Diamond into the palm of her hand.

I watch her, riveted. Trapped inside a bubble of sweet misery with no idea how I got there.

This morning she was my assistant, the same as always.

Now? I'd happily give half my fortune to taste that champagne on her lips and in her mouth. And I'd seriously consider giving more than that to keep her here with me.

Several things hit me at once:

I'm lonely. Sitting across from Bellamy makes me feel lonelier.

The feeling will get worse when she leaves.

And I could do with a lot more of her smiling at me. Exactly like *that*.

But hey. I could also do with a trillion dollars in my bank account, and that ain't happening either.

Since tonight clearly isn't going to be my night on any front, I decide I might as well wrap it up as soon as possible. Stop being such a jackass and let Bellamy go celebrate her birthday with people she cares about. Maybe find something special with the guy her friends plan to hook her up with.

Because that's what she deserves.

And because I can't stand to look at her for another second. Not tonight.

"So," I say abruptly, scooting my chair back and focusing on some indistinct point on the Madeline mural across the room. "We're done. Go have fun."

"That's it?" she says, looking startled.

"That's it. See you Monday morning. And don't think about calling in because you partied too much."

"I've never missed a day of work or even been five minutes late, but I appreciate that reminder to be conscientious and professional. Helpful."

"It's because I stay on you all the time. You're my most reliable employee. I know what to expect from you. I'd like to keep it that way."

I stand and turn away to head back to my original table before she can respond, but not before I catch the funny look on her face.

"You okay?" I say, pausing. "You look like you just caught a bad case of food poisoning."

"Absolutely," she says with a tight-lipped smile that's as authentic as a fourteen-dollar bill. She stands, slings her wrap over her arm and snatches up her little bag. "Because if there's *one* word I want you to think about when you think of me, it's *reliable*."

She sweeps off without another word, leaving me gaping after her while I fight the strong urge to follow her and demand to know what she meant by that. I want to know what the hell's gotten into her tonight. I almost feel like I *need* to know. But then I remind myself of my commitment not to cross any lines with her and thank God she's finally gone. My self-control is running on fumes tonight, and I'm surprised it's lasted this long.

At loose ends now, I returned to my original table.

"Hey," I say.

Ryker, who's still nursing his drink, eyeballs me. "Everything okay?"

"Peachy."

I hesitate and stand there like an idiot, with no real idea what to do with my arms and legs or my body inside its suffocating skin. I don't feel like sitting down for another drink, grabbing dinner with him or going home to read those documents, which is what I really need to do. What I feel like doing is going Godzilla for a minute and destroying all the tables and chairs to burn off some of my thwarted desire and adrenaline surge. But since that seems like a socially unacceptable choice, I decide that the next best thing is to hit the gym and hope I wind down enough to be able to fall asleep sometime before dawn.

"I'm out," I tell my brother. "Heading to the gym."

He doesn't bother to hide his bemusement as I snatch the envelope off the table and turn toward the door.

"You're doing the right thing," he calls after me.

Since that is absolutely zero fucking consolation to

me at this dark moment, I keep going without bothering to respond. I go out to the curb and enjoy the cooling night air on my face. Text my driver. Slouch against the nearest pole and twiddle my thumbs while I wait for him to arrive. Impatiently answer my phone without checking the display when it buzzes, thinking it's him.

But it's not him.

"Yeah," I say.

"I'm not drunk," Bellamy says, catching me by surprise. "I just want you to know that."

There's a new note in her voice, something I can't quite decipher. It seems nervous. Husky. Maybe even a little sultry.

Whatever it is, it makes nerve endings sizzle to life up and down my arms and across my nape. My heart, meanwhile, gallops into overdrive.

"Okay…?"

"I could spend tonight with my friends, but I'm tired of being *reliable*," she continues. "I'm tired of not crossing any lines with you." She hesitates. In the silence, I hear a disbelieving little laugh, and I swear I also hear (feel?) her lick her lips. "I could keep quiet, but I'm really tired of doing the safe thing. And I feel like you should know that the thing I really want for my birthday is *you*."

I freeze, my mouth drying out. Not that it matters, because sudden nerves and excitement lock down my throat and make speech impossible anyway.

"You don't have to say anything," she says quietly. "But I took a chance. I'm upstairs in room 2810. You could come and stay with me tonight. No questions asked. No regrets. And we never have to say anything else about it either way, so it's fine if you decide not to."

I can't answer in that head-spinning moment. Can't

think. Can't breathe. I'd have been better prepared if she'd called to tell me that she's been working under-cover with the CIA this whole time.

"Anyway…" Longest pause of the night. "The ball's in your court, Griffin."

I'm still reeling from her use of my first name for the first time ever when she hangs up without another word.

4

BELLAMY

WHAT DID I JUST DO? Someone tell me, *please*.

Well, I know what. The single most out-of-character act of my entire good-girl life (good daughter, good student, good employee, you name it) and possibly in the history of humankind. That's what.

I'm standing in the middle of the expensive hotel room that I can't afford, reeling from my sudden burst of boldness, when my phone buzzes in my hand. I check the display with a sinking heart, thinking that it's probably Griffin calling back to a) give me my two weeks' notice and b) escort me to the nearest hospital for a full mental health evaluation, but no. It's my best friend, Ella Richardson. Who, I now remember, I forgot to text during tonight's flurry of unusual behavior.

"Hey," I say, huddling inside my wrap and feeling ridiculously vulnerable.

"Where the hell are you?" she barks. I hear a crowd and a pianist playing jazzy tunes in the background. "I thought you said you were at Bemelmans. There's no sign of you."

"Wait, what? I just left. What are *you* doing there?"

"I came to rescue you from the Beast. There was no way I was going to let him ruin your entire birthday like that. Now I'm sitting at the bar with a cake, looking like an idiot. Where are you?"

Do I have great friends or what? Ella is a pastry chef at her aunt's bakery, Valentina's. She makes *amazing* cakes.

"You're the best," I say, my heart aching at the loss of my birthday treat. "Too bad you weren't here thirty seconds ago to stop me from making the biggest mistake of my life."

"Oh my God. What did you do?"

"I gave in to my longstanding crush on my boss, got a room upstairs and invited him to join me."

"What? You're drunk!" she cries, appropriately scandalized.

"Not even a little bit," I say, sad that I won't later be able to pin this temporary insanity on too much alcohol.

"What's gotten into you? The whole time you've worked for him, you've kept your feelings for him under wraps. You act like I'm crazy every time I mention how you make heart eyes at him. And now *this*? What are you thinking?"

I flop onto the bed, which I've turned down in an abundance of optimism, kick off my heels and stare glumly at the ceiling.

"I probably wasn't thinking at all. But if I *were* thinking, it was about how sexy he is and how I'd rather hook up with him than some idiot from a dating app. He should be game, right? He sleeps with every other woman who crosses his path."

"Well, that's true," she says, laughing.

"I'm moving soon. I'll probably never see him again once I go to law school. And I'm twenty-six years old now. I'm so sick of being a good girl all the time. I just wanted to take a chance for once. Do what *I* wanted to do."

"And you want to do *him*."

"Well, yeah."

"Wow. What you just did is either the bravest thing I've ever heard or the most self-destructive. I can't quite decide."

"Neither can I."

"I can't get over this. You and *the Beast*—"

For some reason, the nickname, which he's spent his entire professional life earning, by the way, rubs me the wrong way. Which is ridiculous.

"Stop calling him that," I snap.

"That's what *you* call him," she says, outraged. "Because he's such a jackass to everybody at the office. Especially *you*."

"He's not *all* bad," I say, taking a position based on a gut-deep feeling of mine rather than the historical record.

"Whatever you say, Bella. So is he coming?"

My heart sinks. I have no way of knowing. I may well waste my entire evening up here by myself, waiting for someone who never plans to come.

"Your guess is as good as mine."

"I say give him another half an hour," she says. "And then if he doesn't show—"

Knock–knock–knock.

"Oh my God," I say, bolting upright and getting up. "Someone's at the door."

"It's him!"

"Either that, or housekeeping with a chocolate for my pillow."

"It's him. I know it. Enjoy yourself. Have a fuck for me, since I won't be getting any anytime soon."

"I'll try," I say, laughing. "Gotta go."

I hang up, put the phone on the nightstand, hurry to the door, check the peephole and see that it *is* him. I die a thousand little deaths while I stare at his distorted image and try to decide whether he's come to tell me to get a grip or to take me up on my offer. Then I decide that there's only one way to find out for sure, take a deep breath to steady my racing pulse and swing the door open.

He comes inside without a word, smelling like bergamot and cedar. A warm and inviting scent that has quietly tortured me every day for the last year. And suddenly there he is. My boss, the Beast. As overwhelmingly masculine and commanding here as he is at the office. As out of place in a bedroom of mine as a silverback gorilla at the MAC counter at Nordstrom.

I shut the door, meet his gaze and wonder what the hell happens next.

Tall to begin with, a good six-two or so, he towers over my medium height now that I've taken off my shoes and makes me feel way overmatched. In a thrilling way. He's got all the usual features you'd expect to see in a sex god. Broad-shouldered and slim-hipped with a great ass, he's wearing his work uniform of a custom dark suit and white shirt, although he's stripped off the gray tie from earlier and has it tucked into his jacket pocket. The top button of his shirt is undone now, revealing the top of a white T-shirt and, much more interestingly, the honeyed skin at the base of his throat.

But you're probably wondering about his face.

Allow me to tell you that he's fucking gorgeous.

He's got a halo of sun-streaked golden hair that's much too long. It curls around his ears and collar because he's too busy and impatient to sit still long enough for anyone to trim it regularly. His sleek nose and high cheekbones combine with the divot in his chin to give him insane good looks. The kind that inspire men to march into their plastic surgeon's offices and say, *Give me one of those. Yeah, all of it.* He sports a sexy five o'clock shadow because of course. He glows with health, his complexion dusted with freckles and the slight weathering of someone who spends as much time as he can outside engaged in sweaty activities.

And his *eyes*...

They're the electric blue of the flame on your stove, if someone took that color and purified it, making it so bright that you could hardly stand to look at it. He scowls a lot. You should know that. His lush mouth talks on the phone, makes deals and barks out orders. If you're ever lucky enough to catch him in a smile, you've got about half a second to note his flashing white teeth and dimples. His heavy brows are several shades darker than his hair, intensifying his attention when he looks at you and making you feel as though every interaction is a test that you'd better not fail.

Especially now, when, surprisingly, there's no scowl in sight. Only the relentless focus of a man who likes what he sees and knows what he wants as he gives me a swift and heated once-over.

That is not the look of a man who plans to either fire me or let me down easy. It's the look of—

He's on me without warning, catching me entirely off

guard. There's no greeting. No discussion of terms for this one-off tryst. Just him crossing that line between us and suddenly right there in my space. In my face, where he's never been before, and his extraordinary eyes are the only things I can see. Just his hands on either side of my face and his indistinct murmur of triumph as he leans down to kiss me.

A sweeping wave of euphoria threatens to knock me flat on my ass before I can reach for him.

Oh, *God.*

I'd expected things with him to be next level.

This is next universe.

His lips are velvety and surprisingly tender as they slant over mine, taking control and keeping it. His mouth glides and explores, fitting with mine in every possible combination, each one more exciting than the one before. I cannot respond urgently enough, covering his hands with mine to make sure he doesn't let me go, rising to my tiptoes and surging to meet him. He helps himself to hanks of my hair, gripping it to angle my head the way he wants it. I'm ready when he touches his tongue to my mouth, opening and taking him deep with a helpless groan.

A shudder ripples through his big body, telegraphing the effect I have on him as we mutually help him out of his jacket and drop it to the floor. Which is good, because now I don't feel so out of control for trembling like this and melting down when he touches me. I can't help it that he turns my blood to molten gold when he slowly tugs my wrap off and strokes the sides of my neck and my bare shoulders. No one ever told me that a man's touch could bring me right up to the brink of a screaming orgasm before he ever even approached my breasts or the cleft between my legs.

But he can. *This one* can.

I give my sexual history a solid *meh* up to this point, with fumbling boyfriends who tend to approach, say, women's breasts as cool things to fiddle around with rather than vehicles through which a man can give exquisite pleasure. But now Griffin seems determined to make up for lost time. He sneaks in like a pickpocket, unzipping the back of my dress and easing it down and out of his way before I even suspect anything is happening.

A little shimmy and the thing drops to the floor, where I step out of it and kick it away. The next thing I know, his hands are right there at the edges of my strapless bra, stroking up and down my sides to my hips, ignoring my aching nipples. His touch is languid. Maddening. I endure it for as long as I can, whispering nonsensical encouragement to him with my tingling lips as goosebumps erupt all over my skin, until I can't take it anymore. Shameless and greedy, I grab his wrists and drag his hands to where I need them, flattening them over my breasts in a rough caress.

He takes over without further encouragement, massaging me into a frenzy. I've always been the type of person who didn't want to get too loud in bed for fear of disturbing her roommate down the hall but now, once again, we seem to be making up for lost time. My cries pitch higher when he circles my nipples with his thumbs. Higher still when he abandons my breasts and takes my thighs in his firm grip, hiking me up as though I didn't weigh a healthy one thirty-five on the doctor's dreaded scale the last time I was in for a checkup. By the time I wrap my legs around his waist and he helps himself to my ass on his way to swinging me around and heading for the bed, I sound fully qualified for a role in some adult film.

I don't care. I've waited too long for this moment to ruin it with inhibitions.

Besides, I seriously doubt he'd ever settle for any other reaction from a lover of his.

I stare down at his face, which is flushed and heavy-lidded with passion, and brush my hair out of my eyes so I can get a good look at him and savor this moment out of time. His body is hot. Hard. Imposing. His wavy hair, which I've always itched to touch, maybe smoothing it away from where it falls across his forehead, is wiry but still soft. The blue flame in his eyes burns brighter than usual as he looks up at me. There are striations in them, alternating kaleidoscopes of black and white. His lips are dewy. Swollen from my kisses.

His expression as he lowers me to the bed?

Turbulent. Determined, with the lines of his jaw tightened down. Beyond that? His mood is as impenetrable to me as the Batcave or Wakanda.

He undoes his buttons and sheds his cuff links with unsteady hands as he watches me ease up onto my elbows, then jerks his way out of his shirt. The T-shirt goes next, revealing a delicious swath of that tan skin and muscles that are chiseled and generous without being bulky. He has a dusting of corn-silk hair that tapers through the ladder rungs of his abs—he's got notched hips, I notice with keen interest, although this is no real surprise because he hits the gym at the crack of dawn every morning—and disappears below his belt.

A belt that he now unfastens with lightning speed

before tackling his zipper and shoving pants, boxers and socks down his legs and off.

To my immense relief.

I'm dying to see exactly what he's got in store for me, and I'm not shy about looking.

I get my chance when he straightens and, turning, extracts a condom before tossing his wallet onto the nightstand. His ass? Stellar. His thighs? Powerful. As for his jutting dick, it's long, thick and ruddy as it emerges from a neat thatch of his sandy hair, with a perfect plum of a head. Everything a lucky woman like me could want. I can't wait to feel it inside me, and he can't wait to give it to me. Not if the speed with which he gets that condom on is any indication.

Finally he's ready. We reach for my lacy lavender bikinis together, and I wiggle my way out of them. He pitches them off the side of the bed and starts to join me before getting distracted by the sight of my bare pussy. He lets out a serrated breath and shakes his head as he swiftly looks me up and down, giving me the feeling that he thinks he's the luckiest man in the world.

God knows I'm the luckiest woman.

Since this type of delay is not okay with me, I start to reach for him. He has other ideas. Shooting a dark look of intent up the length of my body, the trails his finger-tips over my torso and takes care to dip them into my belly button, making my hips spasm. Then he lowers his head and gives me a single lingering nuzzle of a kiss that somehow manages to spark every nerve ending in my body. My back arches while the world dims around me and I try to drag some air into my lungs.

But there's no time for more kisses down below.

He stretches out on top of me, staring me in the face

as he settles his weight on his elbows. He's *heavy*. Thrilling. The exquisite sensation of all this skin-to-skin contact overwhelms me and empties my lungs of that last little bit of air, making me gasp. I drag my hands across those rippling shoulders and up into his hair, savoring the feel of him. It belatedly occurs to me that I'm still wearing my stupid strapless bra, and I reach between us, trying to unclasp it. He's right there with me, yanking it off and pausing to rub his palms across my nipples. Some crazy hissing sound of encouragement darts past my lips, and he's only too happy to oblige, working me into a frenzy.

I shift beneath him, getting my hips into place beneath the hard length of his dick. In case he still isn't getting the picture, I cock them and wrap one of my legs around his thigh.

Message received.

He eases up just enough to reach between us and take himself in hand before stoking that sizable head against my slick cleft. I don't see how I could possibly be any hotter or wetter for him, but I guess he wants to make sure I'm ready.

I'm here to tell you: I'm *ready*.

He enters me in a single driving thrust. I cry out, shocked by the intensity of the friction between us. So is he, evidently. We stare at each other for one arrested second, our mouths open while we try to get used to each other and my body eases to accommodate him. He keeps his hips locked, waiting for a signal from me.

I give it to him in the form of a faint smile as I scratch my nails up his back and let my eyes roll closed.

That's all he needs. He begins to move with long and rhythmic strokes that are naturally placed to hit my sweet spot. Every. Single. Time. We fit together perfectly, me arching beneath him and wrapping my legs around his waist as the pleasure spirals lower inside me and concentrates between my thighs. Swear to God, I could live and die like this. I don't need food, water or anything else. Just the magic of our bodies twined together.

I want to savor this moment until our hips give out, but he kisses me again, putting a quick end to that plan. The lush sweep of his tongue into my mouth is more than I can take. My body reaches its tipping point, and the orgasm roars over me and pours out of me on a single high note of astonishment. I stiffen, waiting for the pleasure to wring me dry while he strokes my thigh and murmurs something I can't quite catch.

He goes very still, making me hesitant to open my eyes because I know he's watching me. Worse, I know I'm wearing that sultry glow of a woman who's just had her brains fucked out by a man who now possesses ownership of her body. But I don't even care. I need to *see* him.

So I flick my heavy lids open and discover him right there, his gaze steady and his eyes purest blue flame. Wonder of wonders, a sensual smile even curves his delicious lips before he dips his head for another kiss.

But then he picks up his rhythm again.

By now we're sweaty. Animalistic. Each of his pumps sends a zing of electricity through my belly and makes me gasp and/or groan. His noises are guttural as he works toward his release. Unabashed. He plants his hands on my head and pulls my hair in his frenzy. Thrusts his tongue deeper into my mouth. Smacks my thigh. Grips my ass. Finally calls out my name and goes rigid as he presses his face into the hollow between my neck and shoulder, shuddering against me.

And shuddering and shuddering and *shuddering.*

I laugh, triumphant and undone.

When it's over, he shifts us both to one side, preventing me from being crushed by his weight without pulling out. One of those floating blackout moments follows for God knows how long. I come out of it slowly, spurred by his gentle fingers as they swirl up and down my side, across the swell of my breast and around the edge of my pebbled nipple where it presses against his chest.

Once again, I open my eyes to discover him watching me, unblinking. Both our heads are on the same pillow. His expression is open. Relaxed. There's no sign of the Beast or the real estate titan in his dark power suit.

Only a man capable of surprising tenderness as he smooths my hair away from my temple and tucks it behind my ear.

I wonder if he ever thought of me as anything other than his intrepid assistant before tonight. I wonder what he thinks of me now and whether he wishes we could have more time together. Most of all, I wonder how I can go back to work on Monday as if none of this ever happened.

But those are questions for another time.

If dying while he's fucking me is my number one option, meeting my maker like this is a close second. I could study his face all day and never get bored. I want to know all his secrets. I want to see him smile. I want a million more nights with him, exactly like this.

Don't get me wrong. I'm no fool. I know that every woman who shares his bed (and there are a lot of them) probably ends up feeling exactly this same way. I know there are a lot of women receiving a lot of don't-let-the-door-hit-you-on-the-ass-on-your-way-out bouquets of flowers. I know both that I've just added myself to their ranks and that he'll disappear before the sun comes up. I know that tonight is all I'll ever have of him.

That being the case, I plan to make tonight count.

So I roll over, pushing him to his back as I straddle him. Note the way his eyes widen, and he stares up at me with rapt attention. Lean down for a nipping little kiss that he returns with interest and start working on round two.

5

BELLAMY

MONDAY MORNING SEEMS to come earlier than usual, or maybe it's just that I'm completely unprepared to see Griffin again. I hit the Midtown office at six forty-five, a time when only the first few bleary-eyed folks have begun to trickle in, determined to get settled with my game face firmly hitched over my ears before he arrives after his breakfast meeting. Hopefully around seven thirty rather than his usual seven.

As always, I've got a million things to do before he arrives and intend to start with the most crucial: by heading down to the kitchen so I can grab my first cup of coffee. So it's with some annoyance that I feel my phone buzz in the blazer pocket of my sensible but still kinda sexy peach suit.

It's Ella, which is good, because I've been trying to reach her since Saturday morning.

"Hey," I say, balancing the phone on my shoulder while I pour. "Where the hell have you been? I thought for sure you'd be blowing up my phone and demanding to know what happened the other night."

"I've got my own issues," she says wryly. "I needed time to process."

"Process what?" I demand, reaching for the sugar.

"I met someone at Bemelmans. Right after you and I spoke. We bonded over your birthday cake."

"That was *my* cake," I say, trying to tamp down most of my horrified delight. Ella is no more prone to wild and impromptu sexual adventures that I am. "So who was he? What's he like?"

There's a long and pregnant pause that really spikes my curiosity.

"You tell me," she finally says. "It was Ryker Black. Your beloved's brother."

I blink, my brain blanking out for a second or two. Then it sinks in.

"*What?*" I cry in a scandalized whisper as I dart to the furthest corner of the kitchen and huddle there to make sure I'm not overheard. "Are you telling me you hooked up with *Ryker Black*?"

"*Hooking up* is such a tacky term."

We burst out laughing.

"How was it?" I ask.

"About like your night was, I'm guessing."

"Is *that* right?" I say, trying to keep the smirk out of my voice as I take a moment to enjoy the sweetly lingering ache between my thighs. If *her* night was anything like *my* night, the two of us need to spend about a thousand dollars on joint lotto tickets, because fortune is definitely smiling on us. "Are you seeing each other again?"

"Of course not."

I frown. "Why do you say it like that? Did he escort you from the premises when it was over?"

"No. I left, actually. I stayed until, I don't know, midnight or so. Then he fell asleep, I wrote him a little note and I left."

"Yeah, but it went well, right? What if he wanted to see you again?"

"It doesn't matter if he did," she says. "You know my policy on dating right now. Especially dating wealthy men who are likely to look down their noses at me."

Ella's coming off a long-term relationship with a rich guy who wound up telling her that he didn't know if he'd ever get married. Jackass. Plus, she's got issues with her late father, who was also rich.

"What, you mean going out with some guy you met online twice a month or so? Your policy is stupid," I say. "How about just making it a policy not to date jerks?"

"Since men rarely show up displaying scarlet Js on their foreheads, I choose to eliminate entire categories of high-risk individuals. That's a nice, safe policy. And in keeping with that policy, I left in the middle of the night. Which served the double purpose of preventing any awkward scenes in the morning and stopping me from getting too attached to the wrong guy."

"There's a lot of that going around," I say in glum remembrance of waking up to a cold and lonely bed at dawn on Saturday morning. "Leaving in the middle of the night."

"I mean, that's what you do with one-night stands when you meet a guy at a bar, right?"

"You're asking me?" I ask.

"Good point. So how'd *your* night go?"

"It was amazing," I say. "Like I knew it would be."

"Well worth it?"

"*So* well worth it," I say, unable to stop an embarrassingly dreamy smile and blush from overtaking my face.

"Have you seen him yet? I have a tough time imagining you're going to sweep all this under some rug and keep working together without any issues."

"I get a little reprieve today," I say. "He's not due for another forty-five minutes or so. Time enough for me to work on my acting skills and pretend I'm Nicole Kidman."

"You can do it."

"But get this. *He* paid for the room. I found out the next morning when I went to check out. He had the charges on my credit card reversed."

"Nice," she says. "Classy gesture."

"I sure appreciated it as a struggling singleton trying to make her way in the big city. And there's more. He took my wrap."

"He what?"

"My expensive silk and cashmere shawl that I got myself from Nordstrom. He took it."

"You sure it was him?" she says, sounding startled.

"We dropped it on the floor at the beginning of the night. No one else was ever in the room."

"That's an interesting development," she says. "Maybe he's sleeping with it under his pillow. Getting high off your perfume."

"As if," I say, scoffing.

But there's a tiny part of me—a tiny and stupid part of me—that wants to attach significance to his thievery. Because now he's got a trophy from our night together. A memento. Don't people take mementos because they want to remember something?

"I'd better go," I say when my girlish hopes and dreams threaten to overwhelm me. "He'll be here soon."

"Go with God, then. I know you've got plenty to keep you busy."

"So do you. Go bake those pastries. Don't let the assholes bring you down. Oh, and don't forget I'll be in touch later about the desserts for the Hamptons event this weekend. We can finalize things."

"You got it," she says. "Dinner soon?"

"You got it. Love you."

I put my phone away and decide that my cup of coffee needs a warmup. I've just put it into the microwave and hit the button when I hear a familiar male voice behind me.

"Bellamy. Hey. Good morning."

My heart freaks out, but I quickly rein it back in. The voice is close to Griffin's, but it's not quite right.

Sure enough, I discover Ryker Black when I turn. The youngest and mellowest of the Black brothers, he's got all the outstanding family looks you'd expect.

"Hey, Ryker," I say, surprised to see him because he doesn't normally turn up until eight or so. "What are you doing here so early?"

"I, ah, want to make some calls and get through my emails before the day starts. Thought I'd grab some coffee first."

"I saved you some," I say, watching him with bemusement as I try to picture him and my best friend together. He's not as handsome as Griffin, obviously, but few men are. His brown hair is cut short and severe, and his eyes are hazel rather than Griffin's striking blue. He's got a great smile, though, and no one would ever nick-name *him* the Beast.

"Appreciate that," he says.

We eyeball each other warily as I retrieve my coffee from the microwave and add cream while he pours his. I feel like I should say something, but, notwithstanding last Friday night's events, I'm usually smart enough to stay out of my superiors' personal lives.

"Have a good day," I say with a cheery wave as I head for the door.

"I met your, ah, friend, Ella, at Bemelmans Friday night," he quickly says behind me. "After you left."

I put my responsive grin on stern lockdown (he really liked her; I knew it!) and pivot to face him again, my expression carefully blank.

"Oh yeah?"

"Yeah," he says, a dull flush rising over his face and settling in his cheekbones. He tugs on an earlobe that, I note for the record, is also red. "I thought she might have, ah, mentioned it?"

"I haven't had much of a chance to talk to her yet," I say. Please note, also for the record, that this is perfectly true. And that Ella and I always have each other's backs. And that my late mother, rest her soul, didn't raise any fools. Even if I *do* occasionally sleep with my boss. "Did you guys hit it off?"

"I thought we did. But I didn't, ah, get the chance to get her number. I'm thinking of stopping by Valentina's. Just so I can, you know, say hi."

I frown, oddly charmed by this vulnerable side of Ryker, who usually doesn't have this much trouble getting his words out. I don't know him well, but I'm getting the feeling he's pretty into Ella. And trust me, nice single guys are thin on the ground on the island of Manhattan. Nice single rich guys? Forget about it. Like finding a minotaur sunning himself on top of a Times Square billboard. That being the case, I'm inclined to throw him a bone and ease his way a little bit.

"I'm sure she'd love that," I say.

He breaks into a relieved grin, a beam of purest sunshine. The kind of smile I would kill to receive from Griffin.

"Great. Thanks," he says.

"Don't make me regret it," I warn him.

Hey. He's one of my bosses, but she's my best friend.

"I don't plan to," he says, turning to go with another grateful grin that seems to propel him down the hallway with an unusual bounce in his step.

Also grinning, I grab my coffee and head to my desk, which stands outside Griffin's enormous corner office. I'm almost there when the worst possible thing happens:

The security guard in the lobby downstairs texts me.

He's on his way.

I freeze, the victim of sudden catastrophic paralysis. But this is no time for panic, so I recover quickly and get onto the group chat for everyone on this floor. My urgent goal? To send the alert that I coined myself shortly after I began working here:

GYP.TBIOHW.

Grab your pitchforks. The Beast is on his way.

Like magic, a flurry of activity erupts across the floor. People stop their lazy morning chatter cold and zoom into their offices with the urgency of the Egyptian slaves as they gathered their families close and frantically painted their doorways with lamb's blood before that final plague swept through the land. As for me, I gather the letters and documents that need his signature and put them on his glass and chrome desk along with his schedule for the day. I make another quick trip to the kitchen and back with the cup of blueberry Greek yogurt that he eats first thing every morning and his cup of black coffee. Both also go on his desk. Then I grab his newspapers, my phone, a legal pad and a pen on my way to the elevator. That's all I have time for. Well, that and a few centering breaths to keep me from lapsing into a full-fledged freak-out.

Then the elevator doors slide open and there he is. My boss. Who is now fully cloaked in his focused and forbidding real estate mogul identity and who bears no resemblance to the man who possessed me so thoroughly the other night and whose lingering effects still have my body feeling aroused and agitated.

I go very still as our gazes connect. That split second of electricity as I stare into his impassive face feels like trying to catch a lightning bolt between my hands. It's enough to make my cheeks burn and make me wonder if I can possibly uphold my side of this devil's pact we made. What did I say when I called him with my indecent proposal? No questions asked? No regrets?

Riiiiight. Tell that to my thundering heartbeat.

Luckily, he's already in motion.

"I see the place is still standing, Forest," he says as he gets off the elevator, the same greeting he gives me every morning.

"So far, boss," I say, handing him the newspapers.

He skims the headlines, his long strides eating up the distance to his office as I walk alongside him.

"I'm going to need to talk to legal. I've got some tweaks to the documents I reviewed over the weekend. Damon wants to play squash at lunch, but I'm not sure I can fit that in with my two o'clock meeting. I've been ducking my publicist for a couple days. We need to figure out what she wants. It better not be any more Page Six bullshit about me getting engaged to some woman I've never met. What am I forgetting? Oh, casual Fridays are getting out of hand. I saw someone last week wearing khakis. I hate khakis. No need for us to all look like a bunch of American tourists on vacation in Mexico. Next thing I know, everyone will be walking around in rubber flip-flops. Take care of that, okay? And get me Branson on the phone. I don't like the vibe I'm getting from him lately. I think he's trying to jerk my chain on the deadline."

"You got it, boss."

By now we've made it into his office, where he settles at his desk and reaches for the stack of letters that need his attention. I watch him scrawl his bold signature on the first couple, decide he's done barking out orders for now and turn to go with a surge of relief.

Made it. So far so good. Whew.

"So…we're good?" he asks quietly behind me.

I freeze, stifle a curse and arrange my features into something approximating polite puzzlement as I turn back.

"Absolutely," I say in my crisp professional voice, doing my best to make eye contact for as long as I can stand without singeing my retinas. "Why wouldn't we be?"

"Just…seems appropriate to ask."

A semi-stare-off ensues, during which he keeps watching me with that patented unfathomable expression of his and I begin to feel a flare of annoyance. I suppose he thinks one night with him is enough to make me lose my freaking mind, much like the model he briefly dated several months ago. That nut job once called him thirty-three times here in the office and ultimately had to be escorted from the premises by security. Or maybe he expects me to shrivel into the fetal position and cry my little eyes out, or just be off my game at work.

Whatever. None of that's happening.

"Don't worry," I say pleasantly, staring him in the face. "I know exactly what to expect from you. And what *not* to expect from you."

Since I'm watching him so closely, I have the pleasure of seeing a tiny chink in his expression when his jaw tightens. That tightening jaw makes my day, I gotta tell you.

I walk off, secure in the knowledge that I've had the last word. A feeling that lasts a good, oh, thirty-eight seconds.

Until he unleashes a torrent of work on me, the likes of which I've never seen before and vehemently hope to never see again.

He sends me on errands that take me uptown and then uptown *again* the second I return to the office. Makes, cancels and rearranges meetings and appointments with whiplash speed. Complains about the spice level of the lunch he had me order for him, the air conditioning in his office and the speed of his computer, as if I can control any of that. He has me track down impossible-to-get tickets for the latest Broadway smash when I *know* he's never voluntarily attended a musical in his life. He has me do everything for him but chew his food and flick the pee off his dick when he visits the bathroom, although I suppose there's time for that tomorrow.

By the time the end of the day rolls around, I'm ready to change his nickname from the Beast to the MF'ing

Beast. But do I complain? No. I refuse to give him that satisfaction.

"That's it for me," I call into his office from my desk as I grab my jacket and bag.

He's been tapping away on his computer, but now he looks around at me, frowning.

"Unless you need anything else?" I say cheerily, the same as always.

He hesitates. I can almost see the wheels turning in his vindictive little mind as he tries to think of more shit work to give me but comes up short. Poor planning on his part. He should've paced himself better.

"Nope," he says, equally pleasant. Until he glances past me and gets a glimpse of the extravagant arrangement of flowers on my desk, a conglomeration of gorgeous yellow roses, orchids and other fragrant beauties whose names I don't know. An arrangement that, I'm proud to say, cost five hundred dollars and is *much* bigger than anything I've ever ordered on his behalf before. Naturally, I charged it to his personal credit card. His frown deepens. "What the fuck is all that?"

"My morning-after flowers," I say sweetly. I hadn't planned to do anything so petty, but after the hellish day he just put me through, you'd better believe I plan to stick it to him any way I can. "I knew you'd want me to have them."

I sweep off without giving him a chance for a comeback, the prickling between my shoulder blades feeling a lot like his daggered gaze.

6

GRIFFIN

"HEY, LISTEN," I tell my brother Damon early that Friday morning when I intercept him on the roof of our building, right inside the glass doors leading to the helipad. Tonight is the big annual investor reception out at our family estate in the Hamptons. Like me, he's got his valet bag and briefcase slung over his shoulder. "I need a favor."

He glances up from checking messages on his phone, gives me a closer look and narrows his eyes.

"Yeah, no. I don't like the look on your face."

"Let me take the bird."

"There's room for all of us, moron," he says, trying to edge past me.

I sidestep him, blocking his way. "I'll send it back for you. I want to ride out alone. With, ah, Bellamy."

I try to look casual about the whole thing, but evidently, I don't do a very good job. I find myself getting hot under the collar as I watch his expression slide from confusion to sudden comprehension and then horror.

"You *didn't*," he says.

"I don't discuss my personal life. The point is—"

"The point is, you either hooked up with or plan to hook up with your assistant. Which leaves our company open to a sexual harassment lawsuit. What the fuck is wrong with you? I thought you moved past this. Although, now that I think about it, *this* is why you've been out of sorts all week, isn't it?"

"I have not been *out of sorts*."

Neither of us believe this nonsense. Matter of fact, the last time anyone told a lie this big was back when Cain, noted loving sibling and history's first recorded murderer, told God that he didn't know where his brother Abel was.

"Haven't been out of sorts?" he says, aghast. "I told you the employees all call you the Beast, right? This week, they changed it to TFB. Short for *the Fucking Beast*. Because you've been such a jackass to everybody. You're going to turn up with your head on a spike if you don't change this khaki policy, by the way. And your girl Bellamy is the one who came up with the nickname."

This news bite makes me wince and my morale plummet even further.

"You get your ass sued for sexual harassment, we're not going to be able to find *one* favorable witness for you," he continues. "They all hate your guts. Find someone else to hook up with. Forget Bellamy."

"Don't you think I would if I could?" I snarl before I can stop myself. I have a firm policy against discussing my personal life, such as it is, with anyone, especially either of my brothers, who never hesitate to give me shit about something if they sense a weakness. That's what brothers do. But, on the other hand, it's almost a relief to vent some steam on this Bellamy thing. Maybe give it the perspective it needs. "Do I look happy to you?"

He seems taken aback and eyes me with a new concern, which I both resent and appreciate. On the one hand, I don't look *that* damn bad. On the other hand, I'm a fucking mess and I know it.

The seven days since my glorious and unexpected night with Bellamy have been the worst kind of torture. Honestly, I'd rather have someone clamp my head in a vise grip and be done with it.

I can't sleep or concentrate at work. Can barely eat. I *knew* it was a mistake when I didn't ask any questions and took her up on her too-good-to-be-true offer. I *knew* I already had a banked attraction to her and needed to make damn sure I kept that flame on low. I *knew* that playing with fire tends to get idiots like myself burned.

But I didn't expect *this*.

I see her face. Every-fucking-where. Her luminous brown eyes. Her *mouth*. I live for glimpses of her smile, even if it's never directed at me. I'm like a bloodhound on the trail of her scent (roses), searching it out near her desk and her chair and when she's in and out of my office.

How did I get like this? Will someone kindly explain that to me?

And to think I was naively worried about hurting *her* or giving *her* the wrong idea. At thirty-two, I'm older and no doubt vastly more experienced. I know better than to attach any sort of significance to something that should be purely a physical act. Women tend to get emotionally involved more easily.

And look at me now, boy. Look. At. Me. Now.

I'm a fucking disgrace.

Most shameful of all, I took her shawl thingy. Stole it. Which makes me a thief on top of everything else. I've got it on my bed at home, the closest thing to her that I can get. I'll never tell what I've been doing with it during my sleepless nights. You don't need to know *those* embarrassing details.

I knew this was going to be a one-time deal. I knew I shouldn't play with fire at all but that, if I did, I should only play with it once and be grateful to emerge unscathed.

But that's the thing. I'm not unscathed.

And it's not just that the sex was great. Sex, in my experience, is always pretty damn great. This sex was… It was…

Extraordinary is too big a word to apply to something as natural and commonplace as sex. *Unprecedented* is also too big.

But it was. I'm telling you, it *was*.

The taste of her mouth. Her skin. Her sweet pussy. The *feel* of her.

Am I supposed to forget about all that just because *she* apparently has?

Can someone help me out with that? Because I'm not managing it too well on my own.

Worst of all was that period after, when we just lay together and stared at each other. I know it sounds ridiculous, but I felt a connection to her in that arrested moment. A strong connection.

What the fuck is up with that? I don't connect with people. Nor do I think woo-woo thoughts about *connecting with people*.

But here I am.

Stuck. Miserable. Desperate to spend time with her

again, my condition made all the worse because she's reverted to Forest, my trusty assistant, and hasn't shown me *one* flicker of acknowledgment or lingering interest this week. It's as though she had her moment with me and has now put me firmly in her rearview mirror. I thought I was okay with that. Or could be okay with it, given enough time. But a week has passed and, swear to God, I feel like I'm unraveling. As though I'm one hang-nail away from losing control and flipping desks all over the executive floor.

I can't keep going like this. I need to *do* something. Hence the lies and subterfuge.

Hey. Don't judge. I never said I was a prince.

"Whoa," my brother says, now regarding me with unmistakable concern. "This is worse than I thought."

You think?

"I don't need the psychoanalysis," I snap. "You gonna help me out or not?"

"Fine," he says wearily. "Just make sure this situation doesn't come back to bite us in the ass."

"Great." I slap him on the shoulder, all but sagging with relief. "Owe you one. I'll send the chopper back for you and take care of the carbon offsets."

"Don't do that. Let's try to save some of the environ-ment. I'll just drive."

"What happened with you and the redhead at Bemel-mans, by the way?"

He tenses. "I don't want to get into it."

"Turned you down, did she? That's what happens when you punch above your weight."

"First of all, she did not turn me down." There's a gleam of triumph in his eyes. "Second, I just did you a favor. Seems like you could put your assholery on ice for a day or so."

"Yeah, no," I say, detecting the scent of blood in the water and zeroing in for the kill. Hey, it's what brothers do. Especially when there's something about the vague sadness in his expression. He seems almost…wistful. "You seeing her again? Or did she kick you to the curb on account of poor performance?"

"Fuck you," he says with a little more enthusiasm than typical.

"You're a good man," I say, grinning as I open the door and head out. "I'm sure you'll find someone else. Eventually."

"Fuck. You."

I stifle a chuckle and speed across the helipad, where the pilot is waiting for me and the rotors are kicking up some wind. Bellamy, I see with great satisfaction, is early as usual and already waiting for me inside.

"I'm the last one," I tell the pilot, shaking his hand.

"Okay. A little overcast, but we should make good time."

"Thanks," I say, climbing aboard.

The copter can fit up to six passengers, which means Bellamy and I have a lot of space to ourselves. A fact that seems to give her cause for concern as I get strapped in next to her and the pilot shuts the door behind me.

"Where's Damon?" she demands, frowning. "He was supposed to be riding with us."

I try to look startled by the question. "He said he wanted to drive. Something about saving the environment. He was supposed to tell you."

She blinks, apparently sub-thrilled with this information. "Oh."

With that, she turns to look out her window as we lift off. Which gives me the opportunity to appreciate her up close again, something I've been dying to do.

She's wearing sunglasses, which I could do without. It's hard enough to tell what she's thinking when her eyes aren't blocked. Her hair is in a ponytail, with a few stray strands trailing along the side of her smooth neck. She wears a buttery yellow dress that hugs her curves and looks like distilled sunshine against her glowing skin. Don't get me started on her bare legs and nude heels. Or her subtle scent of roses, for that matter, and the way it wafts in my direction every now and then, keeping me just this side of aroused.

There's no mistaking her excitement as we swoop over the city. She begins to smile, all but bouncing in her seat.

"Your first time?" I ask, grateful that the company coughed up the money for a nice new copter that's quiet on the inside and equally grateful that the pilot wears a headset to communicate with air traffic control.

"It is. You hired me just after this event last year, so I didn't get to go."

"That's right. I forgot."

I lapse into a vaguely troubled silence for a minute, wondering how it's possible that I've worked so closely with her this past year but know next to nothing about her. Other than she loves romance novels. I know that because I see them on her desk all the time. Oh, and she has a dog. I see his picture on her desk. There are so many things I want to ask her. I'm having a tough time focusing in on one thing to start with.

It's getting more overcast. She pushes her sunglasses to the top of her head, much to my delight. I take mine off as well and tuck them into my breast pocket. Then I get rid of the tie and jacket and roll up my shirt sleeves.

Better. Much better. No need to wear that corporate suit of armor all the time.

"You're never going to get me back on the jitney after this," she says happily.

"You spend time in the Hamptons?" I ask.

"Not as much as I'd like. My roommates and I scraped together enough money for a summer share a couple of times, but we"—she turns back to me, faltering as she gives me a swift once-over—"we, ah, weren't big fans of the ride. Or the traffic."

She looks me over one more time, her color rising, before turning back to the window.

Interesting.

"You like the beach?"

"I'm a California girl, so I *love* the beach." She peels herself away from the view, reaches for her briefcase on the floor and produces a sheet of paper. "But we have work to do. You don't want to hear me blather on about the beach."

If she only knew.

"It's fine," I say quickly.

"I know you don't like to get down in the weeds about all the little details," she says, unfurling her paper like it's a map. "But the seating chart is driving me crazy. There're a couple of people who don't really belong at any particular table—"

I scowl. "You sparing me from details like that is one of the top three reasons I keep you around, Forest. Another word and you're fired."

"But—"

"I'm dead serious. Why not relax? Enjoy the flight.

Why be such a workaholic all the time? How do you
expect me to keep up with you?"

"How do *I* expect *you* — ?" she cries, outraged.

"See?" I deadpan. "You're way too stressed."

She chokes back a laugh and puts her paper away,
looking vaguely disgruntled.

"So why law school?" I ask, determined to catch her
with her guard down and break through some of the
barriers between us.

She hesitates but doesn't take long to warm to the
topic. "I like problem-solving. Getting organized and
figuring things out. I love researching things. And I love
helping people. My mother was an immigration lawyer.
She took me to see an induction ceremony for new citi-
zens when I was little. It was amazing." A hint of sadness
sneaks into her expression, but she catches herself before
it takes root. "Anyway, I'm thinking about immigration
law. We'll see."

I have zero doubt that she'd be a stellar immigration
lawyer.

"Didn't you also get into NYU?"

"Yeah. But my mom went to Berkeley, like I said,
and my father still lives out there. I'm an only child.
They were older parents, so he's already close to
seventy. He starting to have little health issues here and
there. I don't like being on the other side of the
country."

Only child. Loving and dutiful daughter. Noted.

"But you like living here in the city?"

"I *love* it. My friends are here. I love the restaurants
and the hustle and bustle. There's always something
exciting going on. I'm really going to miss it."

I silently receive this information the way a patient

receives news that his test results came back normal and file it away for later.

"So why not move him east to be with you?" I ask.

"I'd love to, but he's got his business and employees. He's a landscape architect. He's too young to retire when he loves it so much and too old to rebuild it all from the ground up somewhere else. So…" Rueful shrug. "That's that."

"Huh," I say, not liking her answer.

Not liking it at all.

Not that it's any of my business. But I can't stop myself from looking for loopholes that might keep her here on the East Coast.

Where I live.

"Tell me about your estate," she says, shifting in her seat to face me. "I've seen pictures in *Architectural Digest*, but I'm sure they don't do the place justice. What's it like?"

I shrug and try to keep it moving before the shadows start to collect over my mood. This is not the sort of thing I want to discuss with her.

"It's beautiful, yeah. Your father would love the gardens. Lots of roses and hedges."

"So you spent weekends and summers there?"

"Yep," I say tightly.

She nods, giving me a shrewd look. "I'm sure it was very cool, but I'd think it would be kind of lonely for three little boys."

"Yep," I say again, unable to keep the bitterness out of my voice. "Especially when their mother takes off without a backward glance and hooks up with their father's best friend. And then gets herself killed in a car accident."

"Sorry," she says. "I didn't mean to bring up any bad memories."

"It's fine," I say. I'm having a tough time with the compassion and warmth and those brown eyes as she looks at me, so I turn to stare out my window. I don't want her pity. I don't want her to see me as weak. Anything but that. "Ancient history."

"Well, you win," she says glumly. "You had the worst childhood. There's no way I can keep whining in good conscience about all the times my father forced me to help him weed our vegetable patch. I hope you're happy."

I break into startled laughter, my sour mood lifted in the blink of her gorgeous brown eyes. Caught up in the moment, I allow myself to do something truly stupid.

I face her again.

Our joint laughter converges into something deliciously electric. I feel it shiver across my skin and ache inside me, in my chest and my gut. I feel it as an absolute truth that goes way down deep.

Bellamy and I are not done with each other. Not by a long shot.

Maybe a smarter man would take the time to digest his feelings and formulate a plan without blurting the first thing that comes to mind. But that's the thing about this new phase of my relationship with Bellamy.

There's no place for logic here. It's all about feelings.

"Did you forget?" I ask urgently as our smiles fade.

She hesitates, her eyes widening. "No."

The fact that she admits it gives me courage.

"I know we said no regrets," I tell her, my words spilling out like water over Niagara Falls. "But I regret agreeing to this bullshit arrangement. It's not working for me. You're all I think about. I hear your voice. I feel you on my skin. I taste you in my *mouth*—"

Her breath hitches.

"Griffin…"

"Don't tell me you don't feel *anything*. Don't do that to me."

There's something hopeful enough in her expression as she opens her mouth that I experience a wild surge of excitement. But then she hastily turns away and reaches for that damn briefcase again, producing a legal pad this time.

The only thing saving me from abject despair is the slight tremble in her hands that makes the paper flap.

"I won't force you to go through the seating chart," she says in her professional office voice. "But we have a couple of cancellations. You definitely want to hear about those."

"Absolutely," I say, slumping against my seat and somehow swallowing my impatience even though I now feel sick inside. *Sick*. But this is not all about me and what *I* want. Bellamy is uncertain. I can't blame her for that. She needs time. I can be patient. The thing I cannot do? Let this go. "As long as you understand that this conversation has to happen. Sooner or later."

7

BELLAMY

HE WATCHES me as I descend the main staircase in my floaty yellow gown ahead of the event that evening, making me glad I decided against the standard little black dress I brought as a backup. As a staff member, I'm not required to wear a showstopper tonight. As a woman, I wouldn't dream of letting him see me in anything less. He stands in the foyer below me, strikingly handsome in his fitted black tuxedo. Arrested, he lets his drink hover near his lips. I have no idea whether he's just taking a sip or means to take a sip. None of that matters. All I know is that the touch of his attention is every bit as arousing as if he'd slowly trailed his fingers up the inside of my arm.

And that tonight promises to be magical.

By some miracle, I don't teeter over in my sky-high heels and make it safely to the base of the stairs as he meets me there, having abandoned his brothers and leaving them staring after him with keen interest. Maybe it's my imagination or some trick of the chandelier and candlelight, but his glittering eyes seem brighter than usual tonight.

"Shame you didn't clean up for the reception, Forest," he says for my ears alone. "I was kind of hoping you would."

"What can I say?" I respond, feeling breathless. Dazzled. "My boss has extremely high standards. I wouldn't want to disappoint."

There's no mistaking the desire in his smoldering gaze.

"I doubt he's ever been disappointed in you. He may be a beast, but he's not an idiot."

The B-word catches me off guard, especially at this moment, when I'm the recipient of all his laser focus. I wonder who ratted me out and if I'm about to get my ass handed to me. But he doesn't seem upset. He seems amused.

"Wow," I say as nonchalantly as I can. "What a harsh nickname. Wonder who gave him that?"

He represses a smile. But not those amazing dimples or the telltale crinkles at the outer corners of his eyes.

"I think you know. How do you like your room?"

I'd fully expected to be placed in some austere and windowless room in the servants' quarters, wherever they are, or maybe in some distant carriage house reserved for annoying relatives when they visit during the holidays. Instead, I've been placed in some insane suite with a balcony overlooking the ocean and flooded with bouquets of fat yellow roses.

"I love it. It's amazing."

"That's appropriate," he says, dead serious. "An amazing suite for an amazing woman."

I hesitate, my head spinning.

"Are you flirting with me?"

He shrugs. Eases closer. "I don't know. Is it working?"

Is it?

Of *course* it's working. But I'm terrified to admit it. Terrified to let myself hope for anything more from him.

"Listen," he says, giving me a temporary reprieve from my ambivalence. "I didn't mean to freak you out on the chopper."

"Now you tell me," I say with a shaky laugh.

He starts to smile but it never quite takes hold. Something in his expression is suddenly far too serious for frivolities.

"*Bellamy*. We need to—"

"Bellamy," comes a voice behind me, saving me from myself, this delicious spellbound feeling and whatever ill-conceived confession I would probably have made.

I hastily turn, arrange my features into something slightly less obsessed and try to act like the professional I purport to be.

It's one of the valets.

"I just want to make sure we have the stand set up where you wanted it," he tells me.

"One second," Griffin firmly tells him before I can respond.

"No problem," the valet says, looking a bit startled to be addressed by the big boss. "I'll just be out front."

He walks off, but the interruption has done the trick and brought me back down to earth, where it's time for me to face facts, no matter how painful they might be. I needed the reminder that Griffin is not for me, for a dozen different reasons. He's a jerk a good percentage of the time. He's my boss. He's older and much more experienced. Insanely rich, belonging to this rarefied world where a person needs to pack a lunch before he or she sets out to walk from one side of this monstrous estate to the other. He's a known player who dates models, actresses and civilian women beautiful enough to be models or actresses. He never looked twice at me before this past week.

I, meanwhile, am in imminent danger of losing my head over this man. A man who, while he may be interested in me now, will neatly slide another woman into my spot in his bed (probably while it's still warm) tomorrow or next week.

In short? I must be out of my freaking mind to let Griffin get under my skin like this.

That being the case, I need to give him the widest possible berth tonight.

"I have to go," I say, flustered. "I'm working tonight."

He raises a brow. "Unlike me?"

"You know what I mean," I say, scowling.

"Go. Do your job," he says, then takes another sip of his drink.

Relieved, I start to walk away—

"As long as you understand that we need to finish our conversation. Sometime tonight."

I stiffen, frozen inside some combination of dread and anticipation.

He brushes by me with the final pointed glance as he heads to rejoin his brothers, leaving me reeling with all the implications.

Luckily, I'm too busy to swoon. And this event will wait for no woman.

The next several hours pass in a flurry of activity, with me doing everything from overseeing the caterers and party planner to whispering important factoids about the guests to Griffin seconds before he meets them in the receiving line. My brain is too busy managing all the fine details to allow my personal feelings to interfere.

Until after the guests eat dinner, that is.

When we're all outside under the massive tent that, along with the entire estate, sits atop a bluff overlooking the ocean. The breeze blows. White lights and candles twinkle. The jazz combo mellows everyone out with its take on Motown classics. The guests, nicely liquored now, move freely between the tables, chattering and laughing as they wait for the dessert service, which features Ella's gorgeous pastries from Valentina's. I'm beginning to think that my moment has come to sneak into the kitchen just long enough to grab my own quick dinner. All is right with my world.

Until I happen to glance in Griffin's direction at the exact moment that some blonde sex kitten in a Versace dress decides to make her move and—I bullshit you not—leans in to whisper in his ear while stroking his crotch. I should explain that a) they're standing in a relatively secluded corner between one of the bar areas and some potted palms and b) he immediately says something sharp to her, grabbing her wrist to stop her, but the damage is done.

That knife is stuck all the way up to the hilt deep inside my chest.

Worse, he sees me see them. Probably because my shocked gasp was loud enough to wake the dead. I have just enough time to rearrange my stricken expression into something politely disinterested, walk off and disappear into the kitchen before he can follow me.

My cheeks burn with impotent rage, humiliation and

jealousy. I lean against one of the stainless-steel counters, trying not to get plowed down by all the bustling cooks and servers and to find Ella, desperate to get a handle on my irrational emotions.

"Ella. There you are. Thank God."

Ella, who's dressed in her pastry chef whites, apron and cap and is busy arranging treats on a silver serving tray, realizes I'm there and hurries over. She takes one look at my face, grabs my arm and steers me into the giant pantry, slamming the door behind us and clicking on the light.

"What's going on?" she demands.

"No big deal," I say, annoyed with myself now. This is stupid. Griffin does what I'm sure he always does and I'm ready to drop into the fetal position? Am I insane, or what? "Some woman just grabbed Griffin's crotch. It's nothing. I'm fine. Let's move on."

She pulls an incredulous face. "*This* is fine? You look like you're either going to start crying or grab one of my knives and go cut someone."

"I'm *fine*. I can't flip out every time some woman makes eyes at my boss. Hell, every woman at the party is staring at him and his brothers. They're all blinking out *Fuck me now* in Morse code every time he glances in their direction. And if he decides to fuck any or all of them, it's none of my business."

"I don't know," she says. "I caught him watching *you* earlier. If I had to guess, I'd say any fucking that he wants to do involves *you*. Because he looked all soft and gooey-eyed. But what do I know?"

Hang on. This is an interesting development.

"The Beast doesn't do gooey-eyed," I say, afraid to believe it. It's one thing for him to send me those vibes privately. Something else for them to be powerful enough to be noticed by someone else.

"Yeah," she says flatly. "He does."

We consider each other for a moment in silence.

"He was acting like he might want to hook up again," I confess. "This morning on the helicopter."

"Really?" She claps her hands and hops up and down in what I consider an appropriate reaction to this momentous news. "So what's the issue?"

"The issue is that I don't want to get my heart smashed," I say, annoyed that I need to explain this to her, of all people. "You know I'm not good at casual sex. Duh."

"So get good. This is your chance to practice."

I gape at her. "What the hell are you talking about?"

"I'm talking about you having a little fun. A summer fling before you leave for law school. You both enjoy yourselves while it lasts and get each other out of your systems. Then it ends when you leave. No harm, no foul."

I frown. The idea does have some merit. I'll give her that. My private lady parts are certainly excited about this plan.

"And you're not worried about me getting my feelings all mixed up in this harebrained scheme of yours? Because, I gotta tell you, *I* am."

"No," Ella says with a laugh. "You're going to separate them out. Sex over here. Feelings over there. Never the twain shall meet. Easy."

"Easy for you to say," I say darkly. "I'd better eat. I have to get back."

"Think about what I said."

"I will," I say, and I do.

I think about it when I grab a quick plate of dinner and drink a furtive glass of wine. I think about it when I decide to take a few more quiet moments for myself, head back outside and wander over to the deserted and unlit gazebo. I think about it as the salty breeze cools my overheated face and ruffles my hair.

I especially think about it when Griffin silently joins me at the railing, his earthy scents of bergamot and cedar announcing his presence just before I feel the brush of his sleeve against my bare arm.

My heartbeat speeds up and seems to concentrate at the base of my throat.

"Hi," he says quietly.

"Hi," I say, keeping my attention fixed on the way the moonlight sparkles on the waves below.

"Nothing's going on with me and, ah, that woman. There was, but not now."

I feel a wild and inappropriate swoop of relief. Naturally, I try to put the kibosh on it as quickly as possible.

"You don't have to explain yourself to me," I say with as much nonchalance as I can manage, which is about a grain of sand's worth. "Your personal life is none of my business."

There's a long pause, during which I can almost feel him weighing his words one by one and deciding which ones he wants to share.

"I'd like to change that."

My heart stops as though it's slammed into a brick wall. I make the mistake of turning to face him so I can gauge how serious he is, throwing myself into further turmoil. My gut feeling is that he's serious enough to say or do anything that will get him laid again tonight, but not serious enough to want me to stick around for much longer than that. So I'm surprised to discover him watching me with this quiet intensity, the moonlight concentrating in his eyes.

I want to stand there forever, lost in the possibilities of this one arrested moment, but the jazz combo switches to an old song that's always been a favorite of my father's and, therefore, mine. Natalie Cole's "I've Got Love on My Mind."

Thanks, God. As if I needed anything to deepen my ambivalence or to make this scene any sexier.

He acts fast, probably sensing my weakness. Backing up a step, he extends his hand. I'd love to tell you that I did the smart and self-protective thing and went back to my duties at the party, but I'd be lying. I take his hand. Of course I do. He reels me all the way in. And the next thing I know, we're dancing with our bodies pressed together without enough space between us for a shaft of moonlight to slip through as we sway. One of his arms wraps around my waist. One of my arms goes around his shoulders. The fingers of our free hands lace together. His lips rest against my temple as he murmurs to me.

"I can't stop thinking about you, Bellamy. Does that make you happy?"

Like I'm gonna deny it.

"Yes."

I feel his lips curve into a smile that I wish I could see. "You know what would make me happy?"

"I'm afraid to ask," I say.

"You telling me that you've been thinking about me every second since we were in your hotel room together."

That's the thing about Griffin Black. He goes big or he goes home.

I hesitate, not wanting to give him everything. My

obstinance lasts only as long as it takes him to rub his lips up and down my neck and subtly pump his hips against me, letting me feel the size of his erection. I gasp helplessly.

"Tell me," he says, his lips returning to my temple.

Why lie? It's not like I'm doing a good job hiding it. Why not manage a little grace while I surrender to the inevitable?

"I've been thinking about you. Every second since we were in my hotel room together." I pause, but hey, if I'm surrendering, I might as well *surrender*. "And every second since I first met you."

I pull back enough to look him in the eye. Let him get the full picture.

His unsmiling expression doesn't change, but a tremor of something passes through his big body.

Excitement? Satisfaction? Anticipation?

Whatever it is, I feel it too. I feel it even more when he raises our hands and presses a lingering kiss to the backs of my fingers.

"My bedroom is the one at the end of the east wing. I have to stick around until the last guest leaves, but I want you in my bed when I get there. Waiting for me." He pauses, giving me a swift and possessive once-over. "Don't bother with a nightgown. You won't be needing it."

8

GRIFFIN

I NEARLY RUN Ryker down in the hallway outside my suite in my eagerness to get to Bellamy once the event's over. We have a brief chat. He warns me about getting sued for sexual harassment. We agree that our parents didn't exactly give us workable information about relationships when they scorched the earth during their split, so we're both flying blind with the new ladies in our lives. He expresses surprise about the depth of my growing feelings for my personal assistant.

That makes two of us.

As if I'd risk jeopardizing my work relationship with her if I could see some other way. But I can't. Take my word for it on that. I *can't*.

I ditch Ryker as quickly as I can, desperate to see if she did as I asked.

I catch myself holding my breath as I open the door.

Huh. Funny. *Me.*

King of the one-night-stand and day-after-flowers combo pack.

But once again, I can't help it. It's one thing for me to hope Bellamy comes to my room. Something entirely different for me to discover her asleep on her side in my bed.

As though she belongs there.

I shut the door quietly, eager to savor the fantastic scene as I loosen my tie and work on getting out of these clothes.

She's left the balcony's French doors open, allowing the breeze to filter through the filmy white curtains. The moonlight is bright enough to put a gleam on her hair as it falls across the pillow. Her pale arms and shoulders are bare, whetting my appetite to see what, if anything, she's wearing under the covers.

I walk to the upholstered bench at the end of the bed and use it as a staging area to get rid of my shoes and socks. My jacket, tie, shirt and undershirt. My slacks. Then I walk around to her side of the bed, sit in the reading chair, rest my elbows on my knees, my chin on my clasped hands, and study her face.

Her amazing *face*.

She looks young and innocent now. She *is* young, but I know she can be nice and wicked under the right circumstances. She seems peaceful now, even though she's destroyed my peace in the last week or so. Her breathing is usually even, but I plan to change that. Very soon.

As soon as I give myself a stern reminder.

This woman is not for me. Not in any real sense. At best, she's a welcome respite from the boredom and emptiness in my life. But she's leaving soon, and I'd be a fool to forget that.

I'd be a fool to forget that the only person you can ever count on is yourself. Everyone else? They leave.

Sure, I depend on her professionally. But I plan to keep some barriers up personally. To keep trusting no one. Because if there's one thing I know, it's that women don't stick around, because love is not a real thing. My mother taught me that.

Bellamy will remind me of that lesson when she leaves for law school in a couple months.

Saying goodbye will be painful, no doubt. For both of us, especially considering she's less jaded than I am and has admitted to a longstanding crush on me. A fact that blew my mind, by the way. She's certainly had me fooled this whole time. With a poker face like that? She needs to be out in Vegas making a killing. But the point is, as the older and ostensibly wiser member of this relation-ship, I have to keep my eye on the big picture and main-tain my perspective here.

Hell, even if she stuck around in New York, she'd get wise to me sooner or later. She'd get tired of my gruff bullshit and moody silences. How she hasn't lost her temper with me at the office and punched me in the jaw by now is anyone's guess. But one day she'll have enough of me. She'll give me a big *Fuck you, asshole* sendoff, leave me to my lonely existence and head off in search of some nice guy to settle down with. Which she deserves.

So this thing right here? This ache in the dead center of my chest when I look at her? The unbearable lightness I feel when she laughs with me? The newfound and inex-plicable sense of satisfaction and homecoming I feel when she walks into a room? None of it will last. I'll either destroy it or it will die a natural death when she moves to the other side of the country.

That's the sad bottom line that I need to remember at all costs. Bellamy and I will inevitably go our separate ways. Period. End of our story.

But *I'm* here now. *She's* here now. Even better? She's not wise to me and my bullshit just yet. Maybe, if we navigate this right, we can both emerge relatively unscathed.

The upshot? I plan to take full advantage of the situation while the wind continues to blow in my direction.

That being the case, I take a quick shower and check my condom supply in my nightstand drawer.

Then I slide into bed and spoon her up.

She's thrilling. *Thrilling.* Everything about her wakes me up and makes me feel alive in a way I've never been before. Her warmth. Her nakedness. Her soft pliability as she eagerly snuggles back against me, settling that sweet ass against my crotch. The fresh scent of her silky hair. Her unintelligible murmur of encouragement as she turns her head to receive my kiss. The way she eagerly opens for me, letting me gorge on her mouth as though it's possible for me to ever get enough of her.

The way she surges as though she can't get enough of *me*.

I stroke her with my greedy hands, determined to touch every satiny inch of her skin. Her plump thighs and rounded hips. The curve of her waist. The velvety quiver of her belly. Her narrow waist. The heavy mounds of her breasts with their jutting nipples that feel like raspberries.

Naturally, touching makes me want to taste.

I ease lower, sliding beneath the covers as I shift her to her back and make my way to her bottom half. Her scent welcomes me, that intoxicating musk of fresh oysters and healthy woman. I work my way between her legs and settle in, resting on my elbows and holding a thigh in each hand. She helpfully lets them fall open and scratches my scalp on her way to grabbing handfuls of my hair to keep me right where I want to be.

Then I lower my head and fuck that pussy as best I can with my tongue and lips. And I can pretty well, judging by her strangled cries and the way she arches for me.

I zero in on the hard nub of her clit and I swirl. I suckle. I work her with everything I've got, determined not to stop until she gives me my reward.

And then, suddenly, there it is.

That delicious moment when her body goes rigid and she shouts my name as though she can't help herself. The thrilling spurt of her juices against my eager mouth as she comes for me.

I hold her while she rides it out, rubbing my face against her belly. Loving my way back up her torso, with special stops along the way to suck each nipple and then to press her breasts to either side of my face and smother myself in them for a minute.

By now, she's recovered enough to display her demanding side. Which I *love*, by the way. She levers up on her elbows, her shifting hair and bright eyes making her look wild. Abandoned.

"Stop messing around, Griffin," she says, her voice raspy. "I need you to fuck me."

See? Nice and wicked.

I can't reach sideways for the condoms fast enough, my movements jerky. "As long as you keep calling me *Griffin*, you can have whatever you want."

"Don't even bother," she says, looking heavy-lidded

and a little dazed as she watches me. Her lips, I notice with immense satisfaction, are dewy and swollen from my kisses. Maybe I'm a caveman at heart, but I want every part of her marked because of me. Forever altered. God knows it feels like that's what she's done to me. "I'm on the pill."

Let me pause here to mention that, as a guy with some money who's encountered more than his fair share of would-be baby mamas who'd love to help themselves to a piece of my pie, it behooves me to take the long view and ask a few more questions before I start riding bareback. Or, better yet, to trust no one and just suit up like always.

But an *I'm on the pill* from Bellamy? Music to my ears. Decision made. Done deal. No questions asked.

I flop onto my back and reach for her hips. She doesn't need the encouragement to straddle me. I take my dick—the thing is roughly the size and hardness of a baseball bat by this point—and hold it for her. She sinks onto me as quickly as her tight body will allow, exhaling a raw and sexy *"Ah, God"* when she takes me all the way in.

I'm feeling pretty *Ah, God* myself now, to tell you the truth.

Her pussy is lush and slick. *Hot,* with a grip that says she plans to never let me go.

Fine by me.

I stare up at her, determined to savor this incredible view while I catch my breath for a second. The scene is thrilling and earthy, with something to see everywhere I look. Her flexing thighs braced on either side of my hips. The way my belly rises and falls, tapering down to the place where our groins meet, and the thick base of my dick is just visible beneath her glistening pussy. Her hips and heavy oval breasts. The engorged nipples that tell me just how aroused she is. All that hair as it shifts around her shoulders and falls into her face as she reaches down to lace her fingers with mine on either side of my head. That hint of her seductive and secretive smile, as though she plans to unleash some moves on me tonight that will blow my mind.

I can't fucking *wait*.

"Why are you looking at me like that?" I ask, mesmerized.

"I want to see if I can make you unravel," she says with an experimental swivel of her hips.

"Isn't it obvious?" I say, tightening my hold on her hands as a zing of pleasure shoots straight to my brain.

"We're about to find, aren't we, *Griffin*?"

You know that moment in every old Western movie, where the sheriff vaults onto his horse and spurs the poor beast on so they can chase after the villain like a bat out of hell? That's the treatment Bellamy gives me. This cowgirl of mine possesses a belly dancer's hips. They can pivot. They can circle. They can twerk as though she's auditioning for a starring role in a rap video.

She's fast. Uninhibited. *Relentless*.

And she gives me something glorious to look at the whole time she's fucking me into next year.

Like the way she straightens and braces against the headboard for more leverage, so she can grind harder and while I hang on to her hips for dear life. The way her face twists with gathering ecstasy as her head falls back. The way her breasts jiggle. The way her mouth whispers and smiles and *moans*. The way her fresh sweat makes her face and the edges of her hair damp and trickles between her breasts.

The shameless way she shouts my name and laughs with triumph as she comes and comes and *comes*.

I'd love to draw the moment out and let her savor her pleasure a bit more, but there's no time for that. Not with my heart and lungs threatening to explode. So I do a hard roll and tumble her beneath me so I can take over. Whereupon she whips out a couple new moves on me and shifts her legs to my shoulders before smacking me on the ass. Honest to God, she takes me to a place so deep where the suction is so powerful that the room dims around me. My frenzied pumping falters. I may pass out a little. And the orgasm doesn't shoot out of me so much as it tackles me to the floor, pummels me into submission and leaves me wounded and half-dead. But also happier and more spent than I've ever been in my entire life.

I have no idea how much time passes in that dark space of purest pleasure. All I know is that my soul finally rejoins my body when she shifts beside me, tickling my biceps with her hair when she raises her head, laughing.

I try to frown, but I feel like there's no frown left in me.

"What's so funny?"

"I didn't know I come like that," she says, still laughing. "I don't know what you did to me, but I think I just saw Elvis."

"Interesting," I say, grinning now. "I think I figured out where they hid Hoffa."

Our joint laughter produces an overwhelming sense of urgency inside me. I take her face in my hands and kiss her. Mouth. Nose. Eyes. Forehead. All of that. I would fuck her again if my dick were up to it. I'm so happy. So grateful. So desperate to keep her close while I can. To keep her smiling at me, exactly like *this*. To know that she's not going anywhere. Not yet.

"I shouldn't have told you I've had a crush on you this whole time," she says, looking beautifully rumpled and breathless when I let her up for air. "Now you're going to use that against me."

"No, I'm not," I say. It sounds more like a vow than I'd like to admit, but there's nothing I can do about it. At this moment, I'm positive I'd promise Bellamy anything from half my fortune to a golden phoenix as a pet.

"You sure about that?"

"I'm positive," I say. Another vow.

She nods, looking reassured.

I kiss her again because I can't *not* be kissing her.

We shift again, facing each other with our heads propped on our hands.

"I have a question for you," she says.

"Uh-oh," I say, thrown off by the sudden severity of her tone.

She reaches under her pillow, pulls out her wrap and unfurls it with a flourish. "Is this mine?"

Oh. Shit.

I scrunch up my face and rub my forehead with my free hand. "Any chance we could…ignore that?"

"None whatsoever," she says, trying not to smile.

What the hell. It's not like she doesn't know I'm seriously into her.

I shrug. "I couldn't stand to let you go."

Her dimples deepen until her expression radiates warmth. Steadiness. Complete understanding.

"That makes me really happy."

Good. Because she makes me insanely happy.

"Where do we go from here, Bellamy?"

"Hopefully to somewhere where you keep calling me Bellamy. And keep smiling at me."

I laugh. If only she knew.

"I think we've got that covered," I say, pulling her close again.

9

BELLAMY

I WAKE TO A SUN-STREAKED ROOM, a delightful reminder of last night's activities in the form of the sweet ache between my thighs and a note on the pillow next to me:

Kitchen.

I take a quick shower, grateful I had the foresight to bring my overnight bag to Griffin's room with me last night, throw on a sleeveless blue maxi dress with a nice slit up one side and hurry downstairs. Where I'm greeted by the smell of coffee and bacon and an extraordinary scene.

Griffin. In jeans and a T-shirt. Cooking. And *singing.*

I freeze in the doorway, my sleep-deprived brain too sluggish to process everything at once.

Actually, no. Let's start with his body in those faded and worn jeans that highlight every flexing muscle in his athletic ass and thighs. Let's give honorable mention to the way those endless shoulders taper to a fat-free waist, making a perfect inverted triangle of his torso. Let's give a gold star to his robust arms and the way they fill out those short sleeves.

It takes me a beat or two to shift gears, stop drooling and turn my attention to his kitchen mastery. Honestly, I don't know why I'm surprised that he knows how to flip an omelet in the pan without dropping it on the floor and ruining his breakfast. He does everything else with surpassing excellence, so why not cooking?

And speaking of excellent, what about his voice? I'm no musical expert, but he sounds like a tenor and possesses one of those blue-eyed soul voices that have made people like Ed Sheeran into superstars. His song of choice? My new all-time favorite, "I've Got Love on My Mind."

But the most mind-boggling thing about what I'm seeing right now is the change between the surly and buttoned-up Beast from the office and *this* guy. This guy is mellow. Possibly even happy. *Happy.*

The idea that I might have had anything to do with this transformation is too astonishing to even consider.

He flips the omelet onto a plate, neatly folds it in half, turns to set that plate and another one in front of the barstools at the vast marble island and catches sight of me for the first time.

He stops singing and goes perfectly still as our gazes connect. The power of that connection feels like a blow from a superhero in a Marvel movie, one of those gut punches that makes the villain fly through the air until he's stopped by a well-placed tree and crumples to the ground in a heap. I don't know what to do with this sensation.

I don't know what to *do.*

I'm a sensible person. I know that feelings—true feelings—take time to develop. I don't go around falling in love with men willy-nilly, even men I've had my eye on for a while. But I cannot overstate what it does to me to see Griffin Black smile at me while the morning sun makes a streaked halo of his rumpled hair and turns his eyes to sapphires.

Am I falling in love with this man?

God, I hope not.

"Hey," he says, giving me a swift and appreciative once-over.

"Hey."

"How'd you sleep?"

"Like the dead." Staying right where I am, I put my hands in my pockets and try to focus on a few relevant questions so I don't lapse into full-on simpering. "Hard to believe there was a party here last night. Where is everyone?"

"My brothers are around here somewhere. The caterers cleaned up before they left and most of the household staff has the day off to recover. None of the guests stayed over. I'm guessing most of them are back in the city by now. So it's just you and me."

"Interesting," I say, determined not to set my hopes too high about anything that may or may not be going on here. "So when are you and I going back to the city? Do you want me to grab my bag, so I'll be ready for the chopper?"

"Ah, the chopper," he says, launching into an exaggerated frown. "The thing is…it's down for maintenance. It'll be out of commission for a day or two."

"Oh no. Your brand-new helicopter?"

"Mechanical things. What can you do?" he says, shrugging with what looks like complete indifference.

I decide not to mention that day last month when he threatened to fire me and sue the mechanic who serviced his beloved Porsche but didn't have it finished by the close of business as promised.

"That's *so* frustrating," I say. "Luckily, your fleet has *two* choppers. So when will the backup chopper be here?"

"*Also* down for maintenance."

"Wow. This is beginning to sound like bad luck or carelessness."

"Agreed."

"So what time will your driver be here to take us back? Because I know you always have a lot of work to get done on Saturdays and Sundays."

"Would you believe I gave *him* the day off too?" he says.

I work hard to smother my smile.

"On the very day that both choppers are down for maintenance and we need a ride back to the city?"

"There's that bad luck again."

"Luckily, between you and your brothers there are, like, twelve luxury cars out front. I assume we'll take one of those?"

"That would normally work, but someone slashed the tires," he says gravely.

This time I can't stifle my laugh, so there's no point even trying.

"*Someone?*"

"Me. I slashed all the tires."

We're grinning at each other now.

"If I didn't know any better, I'd start to think that someone doesn't want us to leave the Hamptons anytime soon," I say. "Thank God we still have the jitney."

"Right, but our schedules don't line up with the jitney. We've got too much to get done around here."

"Oh, yeah?" I raise a brow. "What will we be doing?"

"Fucking," he says, staring me in the face. "Getting to know each other. More fucking. Maybe some eating. We'll have to see."

A shiver of anticipation ripples through me. "Ah."

"Unless you have other plans," he adds.

"This is tough," I say, frowning. "Normally I spend my Saturdays doing fun things like washing my clothes and picking up my dry cleaning and grocery shopping for the week. You expect me to drop all of that just for you? That strikes me as very entitled behavior."

"Not at all," he says, those amazing dimples bracketing his mouth. "Looks like I'll have to get AAA out here to replace some tires so we can drive back to the city and fuck and get to know each other in your apartment."

"So we have a workable plan."

"Get over here," he says as we laugh together. "You need to kiss me good morning and thank me for this delicious breakfast I just made for you. I don't bite."

I'm already on my way.

"Actually, you *do* bite," I say, reaching for him. "And I love it."

He sweeps me into his arms, still laughing. I tip my face toward his smiling lips, undone by the rightness of this moment, which feels as natural as slipping into my soft bed to go to sleep at night. Our kiss is tender. Sweetly lingering. When he finally loosens his grip on me and pulls back, he's taken my breath with him.

"Stay here," he murmurs with the velvety brush of

his lips across my forehead. "Spend the weekend with me."

"I thought you'd never ask."

"Will your little dog be okay?"

"Yeah. He's at the kennel. Which he considers a spa vacation."

Grinning, he pulls out a stool for me. "Can we eat now? Now that our omelets are cold?"

"This looks *amazing*," I say, noticing the fresh berries, butter and toast for the first time. All laid out on the most beautiful blue china pattern. "Thank you so much."

"I can't have you getting weak and dehydrated." He heads to the fancy coffee machine and pours a couple of cups, frowns and turns back to me. "How do you take yours? Tell me so I'll know."

"I can get it," I say, startled by this concern and by the role reversal. "I doubt there will be much chance for you to serve me coffee back in the office."

I start to get up—

"Sit," he says sharply. "We can't predict the future. So…?"

"Uh…" I sit back down, bemused. "Cream and sugar. Lots of both."

He nods with unmistakable satisfaction and returns with a perfect cup of coffee for me.

"Delicious," I say. "Thank you."

"Do me a favor," he says, taking his seat next to me.

"What's that?"

"Let's pretend there's no office. I don't want to talk about the office."

"But you're all about the office," I say, startled again.

"Maybe there's more to me." He raises his cup. "That's why we need to get to know each other better."

"You're right," I say, then attack the omelet with gusto. "I didn't know you could sing. Or own jeans."

He barks out a laugh, nearly choking on his coffee. "What are you talking about? Everyone owns jeans."

"But I've never seen you in them."

"You never see me naked until recently, either, but I assume you knew I had a nude body?"

"A very fine nude body," I say, smirking.

"As do you," he says pointedly, making me blush.

"You're going to ruin it if you keep serving me cheesy omelets like this—"

My phone buzzes in my pocket. I pull it out and check the display.

"My father," I tell Griffin, hopping down and hurrying over to the window so he isn't in the shot. "Sorry. Won't take long."

"It's okay. Go ahead."

"Hey, Papa," I say when the picture resolves to show my father wearing his robe and pajamas as he sits at his kitchen table and sips his coffee. With his merry eyes, easy smile, balding head and thick white mustache, he reminds me of a Santa Claus who just had a trim and shave. "How are you? How'd your appointment go? Is your blood pressure still okay?"

"It's fine, it's fine," he says, flapping a hand before squinting into the phone. "Nothing to worry about. Where are you, Bella? Are those roses behind you? Whose garden is *that*?"

"Just a new friend," I say, cheeks burning and uncomfortably aware of Griffin's quiet presence. I certainly understand my father's astonishment at my surroundings. I'm sure the hell not in Kansas anymore. "Do you like the garden?"

"Wonderful!" he booms. "But see those yellow leaves? And are those spots? Tell your friend to check the drainage around there before all those bushes die."

Griffin scowls, gets up and comes to look out the window, taking care to stay out of my father's line of sight. The poor gardener's head is probably now on the chopping block.

"So listen, Papa. Can I call you back later?"

"Sure, sure. I'll be at the nursery for a few hours. I may get a massage for my back. But I'll be home after that."

"Good deal. Love you."

I hang up and discover Griffin watching me thoughtfully.

"My father would lose his mind over your garden," I tell him. "He'd probably ask for some rose cuttings to take back home with him for *his* garden."

"Does he come to town often? I don't recall seeing him at the office."

"Every few months or so," I say.

"When is he due again? Anytime soon?"

"Ah, no," I say, surprised by his interest. He almost sounds like he wants to meet my father. If so, it would be an unprecedented occurrence for this woman whose previous boyfriends made a habit of catching the flu and disappearing for days at a time every time the topic of parents came up. "I'll be seeing him soon when I move."

Griffin nods, his jaw tightening.

My mind shifts to my pending relocation, casting a shadow over the sunny day. I honestly don't know what I'm doing here with Griffin other than setting myself up for enormous heartache one way or the other. Either he pulls the plug on me when his short relationship attention span inevitably shifts to the next pretty face that catches his eye, or the plug gets pulled on both of us when I relocate for law school.

The one thing I can't see happening, no matter how hard I squint my mind's eye?

Me pulling the plug for any reason.

"I thought I'd show you around," he says, saving me from my gloomy thoughts. "You probably didn't get much of a chance to see things yesterday when we were setting up for the party."

"I didn't," I say, brightening.

"Eat up, then."

We finish our breakfast, then make a quick stop upstairs to change into walking shoes. As we start back down the sweeping staircase, it dawns on me that there's a whole chunk of the house off in the other direction that he doesn't seem inclined to show me.

"What's down there?" I ask, pointing.

He hesitates, his expression sour. "That's the, ah, west wing."

"Okay," I say, not liking the look on his face. At all. "Did someone commit a triple homicide down there, or…?"

His expression eases, but not by much. "I don't go down there." Another long pause. "My mother had her rooms down there. Before she, ah, left. A lot of, ah, bad memories."

"Oh," I say, feeling terrible for bringing up this nasty reminder of his painful past. Everyone at the office knows the story of how his mother walked out when Griffin and his brothers were little, leaving their wealthy father to marry his even wealthier best friend just as his father ran into financial difficulties. The tabloids gleefully reported on the story back in the day. I know a lot of the fine details because I, of course, researched Griffin the first chance I had when I started working for him last year. "You know what you should do, right? Do vacation rentals down there. Think of all the interest you'd get if you threw in a free breakfast and Wi-Fi."

This elicits a sharp bark of laughter from him, which is exactly what I had in mind. I'm laughing along with him when he takes my face in his hands and kisses me long and hard.

Once again, he leaves me breathless. When he pulls back and I catch a glimpse of those bright blue eyes, I find myself once again tiptoeing right up to the edge of falling in love and peering over into the other side.

"We're together now. All summer. Until you leave for school. Okay?"

It takes everything inside me not to grin and squeal like I did back in high school when the debate captain tucked a note in my hand after practice.

"That sounds okay to me. Unless..." I furrow my brow. "Did you want to take a vote?"

We burst into joint laughter, followed by another round of kissing. Then he takes my hand and tugs me behind him down the stairs. The foyer spins off in multiple directions. He takes me down a hallway that was closed off last night before stopping at a shut door.

"Let's start here," he says. "You'll love this."

"Hang on," I say as a thrilling thought hits me. "You don't have a library, do you? Isn't that a requirement in a mansion like this?"

"No. Sorry. Billiards room." He snaps his fingers, his expression falling. "That's right. You like to read a lot, don't you? You always have a romance novel on your desk."

"That's okay," I say, doing my best to hide my disappointment. "I was just wondering."

"Ah."

With that, he swings the door open and ushers me into one of the most amazing libraries I've ever seen in my life. Endless windows facing the beach on one side. Two-story shelves on the other three sides. Ladders. Sofas. Tables. Marble statues. A huge stone fireplace.

Books. Books. *Books*.

I shriek with delight, clap my hands and launch myself at him, raining kisses all over his face as he laughs. Until one of my kisses connects with his mouth and the mood abruptly shifts. Suddenly these kisses have a purpose. An urgency.

This elegant and airy library hardly seems like the place for a quickie, but that's the thing about quickies. They can't wait. Griffin reaches around me and slams the door shut, his eyes blazing with passion. Then he backs me against the door and reclaims my mouth. I don't know who reaches for my hemline first, but we somehow manage to get it up around my waist between kisses. We jointly yank my panties down my legs so I can kick them off.

As for his belt and zipper? I let him work on those. I'm too busy staring him in the face as I hook a leg around his waist. He is focused and intent as he frees himself, the hard lines of his face determined as he strokes my slick cleft and murmurs his approval.

There's one second where we adjust, getting our angles right, and then he drives home. I can't stifle my sharp cry, which means it bounces off all the hard surfaces in the room and probably echoes throughout the mansion.

I don't care.

Neither does he, apparently.

He mutters a curse, his eyes rolling closed as he urges me to wrap my other leg around him before bracing both hands on the wall above either side of my head.

I'm ready to go, but he's doing all the work here and needs a moment to adjust to my weight. Or maybe to control the slight tremble throughout his body. He's a big, strong guy, but for a second, I wonder if he's in pain. I have a nightmare image of causing his back to go out and having to explain why when the EMTs show up to take him to the emergency room.

"You okay?" I say.

We're face to face, so I see the exact moment his expression eases past a smile and into a shaky laugh. His lids flick open again, revealing bright happiness.

Possibly even *joy*.

"That's the dumbest question anyone has ever asked me in my entire life."

I laugh too. "Just checking," I say.

"I'm having a tough time getting enough of you," he tells me, beginning to thrust and hitting my sweet spot with unerring precision. "Just so you know."

I wrap my arms tighter around his neck and kiss him again as he fucks me against the door. A far better activity for my mouth than telling him the truth.

I'm having a tough time keeping the brakes on my feelings for you, Griffin. Just so you know.

10

GRIFFIN

I'VE BEEN CURSED by a recurring nightmare for a good chunk of my life. One of the most insidious things about it is that it comes and goes on its own schedule, like a case of malaria. You think that maybe this time it's gone for good, because it's been six months, a year, or four years, and your life seems good, but then it roars back to smack you down again.

It goes like this:

I'm a little kid roaming the dark halls of the west wing, but my mother's not there. No one's there.

I'm ashamed to say that that's pretty much it, but it's enough.

I cry out and startle myself awake to lengthening shadows, a stuttering heartbeat and a jarring sense of disorientation. It takes me a second to realize that I fell asleep stretched out on the leather sofa in the library and that—I check my watch—I've been knocked out for a good couple of hours.

Fucking nightmare. I blearily rub my face and try to regulate my pulse.

Why would it come back *now*?

There's no sign of Bellamy, which is a relief. Nightmare aside, I need time to collect my thoughts and figure out what the hell I think I'm doing with her.

After the memorable interlude up against that door over there, I gave her the nickel tour of the place. We hit the gardens. The stables. The beach. After a late lunch, she insisted on coming back here to check out the books. The last thing I recall is watching her settle in with *Pride and Prejudice*, reading a few pages of my own favorite book, *The Call of the Wild* (I haven't found time for pleasure reading for the last couple of presidential administrations) and deciding to rest my eyes for a minute or two. I'm not much of a sleeper anyway, and God knows there wasn't much of an opportunity for sleep last night.

Now here I am, reeling from Bellamy's powerful effects on my life, much as I'd prefer not to notice them.

She has me doing the following, in no particular order: smiling, laughing, cooking, singing, taking the weekend off, reading and relaxing. Now she also has me sleeping well, because of course she does.

At this rate, I wonder if I'll take up organic tomato farming and pottery if she sticks around much longer.

I don't do change. When you're a little kid and you wake up one morning to discover that your mother has voluntarily walked out of your life, you tend to avoid change the way you avoid sharing your toothbrush with other people. I like my life nice, neat and orderly. If I'm in the mood for change, I can order a suit from a new tailor. Beyond that, significant change gives me hives.

Yet here I am. Slowly transforming into a new person while she's around. Even though I know she won't be around for long.

What the fuck is happening here?

For the life of me, I can't figure it out. Nor can I chalk it up to that honeymoon period when you wallow in an exciting new lover. I've had exciting new lovers before. Plenty of them. None of them have made me feel like *this*.

To make matters worse, I can already feel the gloom from our pending separation gathering over my head. Not the separation coming in the fall. I don't want to think about *that* yet.

No, I'm talking about the separation looming sometime tomorrow when we exit our perfect bubble here in the Hamptons and return to the city and our regularly scheduled lives. Much as I hate to admit it, I'm missing her already. I've gotten used to having her at arm's reach. I like knowing she's in my bed and will be there the next time I reach out for her or wake up in the morning. I have no idea how much time she'll want to spend together once we go back home, or whether we'll spend our time in my apartment or hers. As for the question of how we're going to hide our relationship in the office, I have no clue. I've got a decent poker face, but my self-control is sorely lacking where she's concerned. Every time I look at her these days, I'm sure it's with those zinging heart eyes you always see in old cartoons. So I'm betting it's only a matter of time before our relationship gets outed, one way or the other. Which, of course, puts me and the company at risk of some sort of sexual harassment lawsuit.

But I'm already at risk, aren't I?

And the risk with Bellamy feels like it has nothing to do with anything going on at the office and everything to do with the growing ache inside my chest.

A smart man would mitigate any potential damage by ending things at the conclusion of the weekend. The world is littered with bosses and employees who enjoy casual affairs at, say, conventions or trade shows. This could fall into that category except for one small problem.

I'm not fucking doing that. I've already tried the one-and-done strategy. It didn't work. I'm smart enough to learn from my past mistakes, and it was a mistake to think that I could work her out of my system that easily. The upshot? I'm not giving Bellamy up one second sooner than I need to, and even then, it's not looking good.

So where does that leave me?

It leaves me needing to take it down a notch or two. We're having a casual affair. Enjoying each other's company within a few clearly defined limits—namely that this relationship is never going to go anywhere. Like I mentioned before, even if she wasn't moving to the opposite coast, she'd get sick of me and my assholery soon enough. A good woman like that deserves a good man. Which means she doesn't deserve me.

A *casual affair*.

Nothing more. Nothing less. Maybe we'll see each other during the week. Maybe we won't. Maybe we'll grab dinner sometimes. Maybe we'll be too busy for that. No big deal either way. That's the thing about casual affairs: they're *casual*.

The one thing I'm not going to do—the thing I can never allow myself to do—is get all wrapped up in Bellamy or any other woman. I don't need the hassle, and I damn sure don't need the heartache of letting someone in when they're probably going to leave. Look at what happened to my father. Hell, that poor schmuck received a solemn vow in a church before God and everybody, yet he still got his guts ripped out. Bellamy hasn't made me any vows. She never will.

The bottom line is that we can enjoy each other and have fun while it lasts knowing it won't last for long. One night wasn't enough. The rest of the summer will have to be. Because she isn't mine to keep. I'll be fine if I remember that and keep it *casual*.

My plan firmly in place, I head out to the foyer and listen for signs of life. The house is quiet, but delicious scents drift down the hallway, leaving me no choice but to follow my nose to the kitchen, where I get a nice surprise. The breakfast table is set for romance. Flickering candles. Sparkling goblets. An open bottle of red wine. Flowers. Baked manicotti sits in its covered dish atop the stove, making my heart sing.

But no Bellamy.

The doors leading to the deck overlooking the ocean are open, though, so I peek outside to see if there's any sign of her. And there she is at the railing, staring out at the fiery sunset and the clouds blowing in on the horizon, the breeze ruffling her hair.

"Hey," I say, a smile creeping across my face. I'm beginning to think that she keeps all my smiles in her back pocket and only doles them out when she's nearby. "You didn't have to do all that—"

She hastily ducks her head and wipes her eyes, but not before I catch the sparkle of tears.

Everything inside me turns to ice. I'm just getting used to Bellamy being my sunshine. I didn't think clouds would pop up so soon and with zero warning.

Besides, my mother cried the last time I saw her. The memory barges in, startling me with its clarity.

"What's wrong, Mommy?" I said, yawning.

"Griffin," she said, hastily ducking her head, wiping her eyes and getting up in what I now realize was an attempt to hide the open suitcase on her bed. "What're you doing up this late?"

"I'm thirsty. Do you need a hug?"

Watery smile from my mother as she reached for me. "I would love a hug, my sweet boy. Mommy loves you. Don't forget that."

Mommy loves you. What a lie that was, eh?

She's been gone ever since the following morning and my life has never been the same.

And I hate to see women cry.

"What's wrong?" I ask Bellamy sharply.

"I'm okay," she says, waving a hand. She seems embarrassed. "It's nothing."

"Then stop crying. What do you need?"

That's the problem-solving portion of my brain talking. If Bellamy needs something, I'm on it. I have the money and resources to buy, find, build, order, hunt or steal whatever she requires. I'd prefer not to get into any criminal enter-prises, but if someone has hurt her or she needs someone taking care of, I know a guy who knows a guy. Whatever it takes to make her (and me, by extension) okay again.

"Nothing," she says, looking a little startled by my vehemence as I join her at the railing. "Unless you know how to resurrect my mother so I can wish her happy birthday?"

There it is. My worst nightmare. A problem I can't solve for her.

"Your...mother?"

"Yeah." She wipes another tear, leaving a wet spot on her cheek. "It's been five years."

I stand there waging a silent battle between my sudden paralysis and my overwhelming curiosity about every aspect of her life. I *just* swore to myself that I'd keep things casual with Bellamy. I don't do emotions. I damn sure don't do *mothers*. Mothers are my personal kryptonite. I'd rather submit to an IRS audit of my personal and corporate finances for the last five years than discuss my own personal mother situation.

But…

If Bellamy needs something, I have to ferret it out and make sure she gets it. I'm not sure when exactly I undertook this responsibility, but it feels like a blood oath. A solemn vow as a man. I have to take care of her. In this case, she may need a sympathetic human being to talk to, but it's her bad luck that I'm the only person available. Sort of like needing a blood transfusion only to discover that the only available person is a cyborg.

Still, I can do my best.

"Do you…want to talk about it?" I ask carefully.

Magic words, apparently.

"She died when I was in college. Right before winter break. I'd just finished up my finals and was getting ready to go home for Christmas. She had a car accident."

I nod, incapable of mentioning that my mother walked out on us just after Christmas.

And died a few months after. In a car accident.

"I'm not a big fan of the holidays anymore," she says ruefully.

You and me both, sister.

"And you know all about terrible car accidents, don't you?" she says. "I read somewhere that it takes at least three years to get over a big shock like that. I'm not sure I'm over it now."

I nod, my lips twisting with the effort of swallowing back some of the emotion that seems determined to rise in my throat. I had no idea that Bellamy and I had so much in common. I also have no idea what to do with this new knowledge. And I doubt that my sphinx routine is helping her in her time of need.

"Anyway," she says quietly, turning back to the sunset and giving me a reprieve from the heartbreak in those big brown eyes. "I was just standing here thinking how much she would have loved your view. She loved the ocean. And then I remembered that today is her birthday. I've been so busy with you that it slipped my mind. Which makes me feel like a bad daughter."

"You're not a bad daughter," I say. "You're human."

"You think?" she asks, brightening.

"Yep."

"It's kind of strange, isn't it? The way we both abruptly lost our mothers?"

I'm having a tough time breathing. It takes me a long beat or two to dredge up an answer.

"I don't talk about my mother."

"Oh," she says lightly. "Ever?"

This is tiptoeing around the edge of talking about her, so I decide to infuse more steel into my voice.

"Not if I can help it. I also don't do emotions." My voice gets gruffer by the syllable. "So you've got the wrong guy if that's important to you."

One of her brows hikes up. "I've got the wrong guy if it's important to me to occasionally engage in basic conversations about my life?"

I decide that this is as good a time as any to outline

the parameters of this casual relationship. Make sure we understand each other.

"That's right. I'm good at sex. The occasional dinner. I can be generous with my money." I pause to clear my tight throat. My intention was to give her a hard stare while I made my little speech, but I discover I'm having a tough time getting the words out while looking her in the eye. "That's all there is to me. I'm a workaholic. You know that. I'm not good at relationships or feelings. Just so we're clear on what to expect from each other."

She stares at me, expressionless and unblinking.

"I see," she says when the ringing silence turns awkward. "Thanks for the heads-up. So I need to be one hundred percent sex machine at all times when we're together and zero percent actual human woman whose feelings sometimes seep out. Is that what you're telling me?"

I don't appreciate the sarcasm. I'd thought it was a decent speech.

"Pretty much, yeah," I say, beginning to feel sheepish.

"Good to know." She gives me a tight smile as she brushes by me on her way back inside. "I wish you'd mentioned that before I went to the trouble of making this delicious manicotti dinner. Now I'll have to eat it by myself."

"Huh?"

She grabs a long and hairy-looking knife from the magnetic block on the wall and starts slicing a crusty loaf of bread. The sight of it, along with the savory scent of the manicotti, makes my mouth water as I follow her and shut the door behind me

"Dinner is a shared activity for people who want to get to know each other better. That's clearly not *you*. So you can vacate the kitchen while I eat, then come back later for, I don't know, a peanut butter and jelly sandwich or something."

"You're kidding," I say.

"I'm *not* kidding."

"It's my food. In my kitchen. In my *house*!"

"I don't know what to tell you," she says, leveling her murderous gaze on my face. "But you're not eating one bite of this food."

Something in her quiet voice—a note of demonic possession, maybe—strikes terror in my heart and freezes me where I stand.

Dumbstruck, I watch as she removes my place setting from the table and, making a real production out of ignoring me, serves herself wine, manicotti and bread. Oh, and she made a nice salad, too. Part of me wants to laugh. Part of me wants to demand to know what the hell she thinks she's proving here. A bigger part of me wonders why I can't keep my fucking mouth shut more of the time.

"Okay," I finally say as she sets her plate on the table and reaches for her wine. "Can I grab my food now? You've made your point."

To my absolute astonishment, she lowers the glass from her lovely lips, flashes me a chilling smile and uses her free hand to take that knife and jam its tip into the cutting board.

"I don't think I *have* made my point," she says, casually gripping the hilt as that knife stands upright. "I would rather pack all this food up and drive it to the nearest food pantry than give you any. I would rather throw all this food into the ocean and let the fish eat it than give you any. Matter of fact, I would rather binge-eat all this food, vomit and then eat all the vomit than give you any. Just so we're clear on what to expect from each other."

A standoff ensues. I debate whether to just grab a plate and take my chances. The manicotti looks and smells delicious, and I've got several inches and probably a good fifty to seventy-five pounds on her. I could probably take her.

On the other hand, the steely glint in her eyes perfectly matches the knife's blade. I don't *think* she'd slice me open like a freshly caught trout she plans to cook for dinner, but I don't particularly want to find out.

Oh, and by the way?

I've never been more fascinated—and aroused—by a woman in my life than I am engaging in this battle of wills with Bellamy.

I usually get what I want, but I'm willing to strategically lose a minor battle here or there to make sure I win the war.

In this case, I want the manicotti, sure. But I *really* want Bellamy. I'll sacrifice the one to make sure I don't lose the other.

"Have it your way," I say, shrugging. "There's other food. Enjoy."

"I will," she says sweetly. "I'm a great cook. Not that you'll ever find out."

I shrug again as I make my way toward the hallway, giving her plenty of time to change her mind and call me back—

"Griffin," she says behind me.

See? It worked.

Stifling a smile, I turn back and try to look politely puzzled.

"Can we leave early in the morning?" she says coolly, making my hopes plummet through the floor. The unexpected boom of thunder outside punctuates the end of her sentence and makes things a million times worse. "I've got a lot of stuff to do before work on Monday."

I stare at her, listening to the sudden sound of rain driving against the house and fearing that I may have met my match. God knows I lost that round, and worse, I have absolutely no idea how to get myself back on the playing field.

11

BELLAMY

I HEAR him outside my room around eleven o'clock that night, prowling up and down the hallway. I've been reading *Pride and Prejudice* in bed, but now I glance up, listening. I'm sure he thinks he's panther-like as he pads around in his bare feet, but the sound is loud in the house's relative silence now that the storm outside has passed.

The storm *inside*? Not so much.

I'm still pissed. *Pissed.* A more evolved person would call him into the room for a mature discussion about the state of their relationship and the need for better communication. Me? I'm staying right where I am. I could've rejoined him in his room and ignored him down there just as well, but this is much more satisfying. Let him come to me. He can pace that hallway until he wears out the floor and crashes through to the foyer for all I care.

Silly? Spiteful? You betcha. I'm still not moving.

Don't get me wrong. I know we're engaged in a power struggle here. I also know that power struggles waste valuable time and are destructive to relationships. I may be young, but I'm no dummy. It's just that I absolutely cannot shake the feeling that there's much more at stake here than me punishing him for being an asshole. Hell, his gruffness is no big surprise. I've known about it since day one. And it's not as though I thought that a few bouts of mind-blowing sex would eradicate that part of his personality forever.

Like I said, I'm no dummy.

It's just that I feel a little bit like Dorothy when she sees behind the great and powerful Oz's curtain and realizes that there's a flesh-and-blood man hidden back there. Griffin is a great and powerful real estate titan. He's an intimidating boss. And yeah, he's a jerk a significant percentage of the time. But now I've peeked behind his curtain and seen hints of the man I think he keeps trapped back there. I've seen that man's humor. His tenderness. His thoughtfulness. His surprising vulnerability. These glimpses of that hidden man shake me to my core. They *touch* me. The asshole is a lot like the great and powerful Oz. He's got power and bluster on his side. Sleights of hand designed to direct my attention away from his hidden man. He keeps frantically adding panels to that curtain faster than I can tear them away. And that's his job, I suppose. He's only protecting his status quo. Anyone would.

But I've seen that hidden man. I want more of him. Maybe even need him. Matter of fact, my growing feelings for him have generated a surprising protective streak that requires me to do whatever it takes to protect him, even if the protection he needs is from himself. Because I don't think that Griffin the asshole is happy. Not really. But this other man I keep glimpsing? He could be happy. And I could be happy with him. Under the right circumstances.

What are the right circumstances? No idea. But I'm determined to figure it out.

By the way, I'm fully aware that I'm the embodiment of one of *Cosmopolitan* magazine's Relationship Don'ts right now. Don't go around falling for jerks. Don't make the mistake of thinking you can change them into princes. Don't delude yourself into believing that the love of a good woman is all they need.

I know, I know.

Believe me, if I had a sister who turned up with a relationship problem like mine and found herself falling for a Griffin Black type, I'd tell her to R-U-N and never look back—

Huh.

Maybe I *am* a dummy after all.

Because I'm damn sure not going anywhere, am I?

I can't. I won't.

Ridiculous as it sounds, I feel like something huge is at stake here for both of us. Something worth fighting for. That's why I can't give in and let him bulldoze me. Not this time.

I find myself holding my breath when his footsteps stop outside my door. And breathing again when he lets himself in without knocking a few seconds later.

I shoot him an unsmiling glance as he shuts the door, noting the color rising over his bare torso and neck and settling in his cheeks with great satisfaction. His expression? Grim. He's showered and ready for bed, wearing a pair of low-slung cotton pajama bottoms that hover around his notched hips. He brings his wonderful scents of bergamot and cedar with him as he comes closer, throwing my equilibrium further off kilter. He climbs into bed beside me, gives his pillows a couple of whacks and settles in with his arms resting behind his head.

He says nothing.

I say nothing.

He adjusts the covers.

I idly turn the page in my book and try to get into the chapter. Oh, look. Mr. Darcy is *also* a jerk.

Griffin clears his throat.

Everything inside me waits at full attention.

"I prefer to watch the news before bed," he says. "Just FYI."

"Thank you for that information," I say, flipping another page. "I was *just* sitting here wondering about your bedtime routine."

He huffs out one of those long sighs of boredom.

"What am I supposed to do here? *My* book is all the way downstairs. And I don't want you threatening me with a knife again, so I can't turn on the TV."

I wordlessly pass him his book, which I'd brought up earlier and placed on the nightstand just in case. Hey, you don't spend a year working as Griffin's personal assistant without learning a few pro tricks.

He makes a disbelieving sound, takes the book and tosses it to the end of the bed.

"You sure know how to ruin a perfectly good Saturday night," he says.

That comment warrants me putting down my book long enough to shoot him a sidelong glare.

"*You* are a bully who keeps his feelings bottled so deep inside that it's a wonder they don't ooze out of your pores."

"*What?*"

"You heard me," I say, returning to my book. "Someone needs to break you of all your bad habits."

"I guess *you're* the person," he says, sounding incredulous.

I lower my book again. Think about it. Shrug.

"If it's not me, I just hope I live long enough to see who it is."

I'm about to continue pretending to read when he snatches my book and tosses it to the end of the bed, where it lands on top of his.

"Those are first editions," I say, outraged.

"How long are you going to keep giving me shit for what I said?" he demands, eyes flashing.

"No idea. How long are you going to keep acting like such a jackass?"

A long and seething moment passes between us. It's a wonder the toxicity doesn't rot the beautiful linens.

"Just so you know, this is normally the moment in a relationship when I start blocking numbers and having you send goodbye flowers," he tells me, his jaw tight.

I freeze, itching for the feel of that knife again.

Now seems like a good time to mention that I'm normally a very low-key and nonviolent person. I'm slow to anger. Quick to forgive. I don't let much ruffle my feathers. That's why my sudden volcanic rage is so significant.

I think about the special moments we've shared, in bed and out, and wonder if he makes every woman he's with feel the way he makes me feel. I think about all the flowers I've ordered over the past year and the faceless and presumably sad women behind those flowers. I decide that come hell or high water, no matter what else ever happens between us, he will *not* lump me in with everyone else.

I get out of bed without a word and head straight for the door, treating him to the sight of me in my filmy white tank top and bikinis as he gapes after me.

"I'm on it, boss," I say, yanking the door open for him. "I think I'll order myself some orchids this time. Have a great night."

"Are you serious?"

"Have a great night."

Scowling, he gets up and stalks over to the door, looming over me. "I'm not leaving."

"Yes, you are." I can barely get the words out. "Get the fuck out."

"Stop being such a hothead!" he roars, leaning past me to slam the door shut again. "I'm trying to apologize! Why can't you give me half a chance?"

"I have seen zero signs of an apology from you," I say, startled by this information.

"That's because I'm not good at it!"

Truer words were never spoken.

I take a moment to catch my breath. Then I give him the floor with a sweeping gesture before folding my arms over my chest and hiking up my chin. "Let's hear it."

"Jesus, Bellamy," he says, running his hands over the top of his head and ruffling his hair. "Can you make this a *little* easier for me?"

"No," I say flatly.

He shakes his head and mutters something indistinct before looking to the ceiling as though he needs divine intervention. Little does he know that *I* am also sending up a prayer for lightning to strike him right in his fat head as punishment for being the most infuriating human being I've ever met.

"Look," he says quietly, lowering his hands. "I've been gruff pretty much my entire life. I'm not great at communication. I don't let people in. You know that. That's why you call me the Beast behind my back."

I nod impatiently. I'm tempted to give him shit about this non-apology apology, but I decide to let things unfold for a minute.

Something softens in his expression, steadily warming up his face until his blue eyes seem to glow as they look at me. And I feel a responsive tug deep in my belly.

And in my heart, if I'm being honest.

"But it might be time for me to see if I can do better. We're not going to have that much time together. I don't want to waste it on my twisted bullshit."

"Don't say that. You're not twisted," I say. "And I don't want you to think that I expect you to spill your guts just because I share something with you. But you can't freak out and push me away every time the topic of mothers comes up."

"My mother took everything that was good and possible in my life and fucked it up when she walked out." For a fleeting second, I get a heartbreaking glimpse of the little boy he must have been back then, lost and vulnerable. Bleak. "Am I a grown man now? Yeah. Is that the kind of thing you get over? Not really. It pops up on Mother's Day. And her birthday. And Christmas. And when other people talk about how great *their* mothers are. And when it comes to me opening up about my feelings. And *that's* all you need to know when it comes to me and mothers."

"I'm sorry that happened to you," I tell him from the bottom of my heart.

"Yep," he says tightly.

There's a pause.

"Don't look now," I say, trying to hold back the smile that wants to break through. Now isn't the time. I know that. But I also know a breakthrough when I see one. "But I think you just opened up a little bit. How do you feel?"

He blinks and furrows his brow, making a show of thinking it over.

"Shaky. Also lightheaded." He gives me a doleful look. "But that probably has to do with being starved half to death, since I didn't get any dinner."

Well, what can I say? He got me.

I burst into laughter. He quickly joins in and reaches out for me, reintroducing sunlight to my world. He takes my hand and reels me in until I'm hugged up to the warmth of his strong body, a place that probably feels more like home than it should.

"Funny," I say, clinging to his shoulders while he tunnels his fingers through my hair and rains kisses on my face. "I never heard the word *sorry* come out of your mouth."

"Too late now," he says smugly. "I got myself out of the doghouse without it."

"True."

I laugh until his lips find mine and put my mouth to better use. I'm breathless when we pull apart. Triumphant. I know I only emerged the victor from this one small battle, but it sure feels like a significant step toward winning the war for his feelings. I can't help but notice that a certain part of him seems incredibly happy to be reunited with me. I reach between us, determined to give him an experimental rub or two.

"Not so fast," he says, gripping my wrist. "I know you can't keep your hands off me, but I'm on strike until you feed me my dinner."

"Oh my God," I cry, wondering when I've seen a bigger baby. "Will you move on?"

"*No*. I'm starving. And that manicotti looked delicious. You'd better not have eaten it all, either."

"Poor Griffin." I smile up at him, smoothing the hair away from his temples the way I would a child's. "I hope you can forgive me for Manicotti-Gate one day."

I start to lead him toward the door, but he keeps a firm grip on my waist, stopping me. I turn back, ready to ask him what's wrong, but the sudden blazing intensity in his eyes stops me.

"I'm crazy about you," he says, his voice husky. "In case you didn't know. I'm really crazy about you."

"Good," I say, even though this whole thing feels way too big for me and moves much too fast. The thing I can't quite figure out is why I'm so determined to let it all play out. I'm not sure if I have any self-protective instincts left when it comes to Griffin Black. "I'd hate to think I'm in this by myself."

12

GRIFFIN

"GRIFF? YOU WITH US?" Damon says to me at the meeting in the conference room Monday morning.

Startled by this mention of my name, I look up from where I've been doodling on my legal pad and discover my brothers and the lawyers all staring at me as though I've suggested relocating the entire operation to a yacht anchored off the coast of Tahiti. I hastily clear my throat, sit up straight and try to act like I've had my bleary head in the game for the last forty-five minutes.

"Absolutely," I say, closing my leather folio in the hopes that no one will see the entire page full of scribbles. I don't *think* I've been writing Bellamy's name with little hearts around it, but in my current semi-obsessed state? You just never know. While I'm at it, I also hope that no one has noticed that my attention has been riveted on the elevators on the other side of the glass wall (still no sign of her; her dentist appointment must be running long) or that I've checked my watch approximately ten thousand times since this endless meeting began. "I'm just going to grab some coffee."

Ryker leans forward and eyeballs me with amusement down the length of the huge table. "Are we keeping you from something? I get the feeling you're distracted."

I try to look politely puzzled by this suggestion while simultaneously shooting him a discreet *shut the fuck up or prepare to die* glare.

"Not at all," I say as I get up and head to the side table for a refill, keeping one eye on those elevators. "Continue."

One of the lawyers resumes droning about a zoning issue we've been trying to resolve—luckily, lawyers are good at droning—freeing me up to keep wallowing in my thoughts.

About Bellamy.

She's seriously screwed with my head, that one.

I'm in bad shape, man.

Bad.

Shape.

I take a fortifying sip of coffee, resume my seat at the table and flip to a new page in my legal pad. As someone who prides himself on being clearheaded, logical and organized, I wonder when and how I've turned into this sappy mess who's so hopped up on hormones and adrenaline that he can barely sit still or concentrate while waiting for a glimpse of his crush.

Well, I know, don't I?

After Saturday night's big talk and manicotti (delicious, by the way; she's an amazing cook), we retired to her room. Once there, according to my best and most conservative estimates, we engaged in seventy-five percent of the positions in the *Kama Sutra* and got only fifteen minutes of sleep the entire night. My dick is sore and probably needs to be seen for a hydrating trip at the nearest clinic, so I can only imagine how *she* feels.

Although, judging from the scratches across my back, her enthusiastic cries and coos and the sultry and satisfied smile she wore the last time I made her come, she's not complaining. At all.

Yesterday morning, we got up. Showered together. Ate. Packed up and flew back to the city in a thoughtful silence, although we *did* hold hands the entire way.

"Grab some stuff," I told her when I pulled up in front of her apartment building to drop her off early in the afternoon. Why? Because I couldn't stand the idea of letting her go and ending our idyll. Still can't, to be honest. "Stay with me."

Note that my mouth was dry and my heart damn near pounded out of my chest when I said it. Also note that I didn't say, for example, "stay with me tonight," or otherwise put any limitations on her "staying with me," a detail that I personally find astonishing. As someone who's enjoyed his share of weekend getaways with lovers over the years, I've always found that twenty-four to forty-eight hours is more than enough time for even the sexiest and most intriguing woman to become annoying. This interlude with Bellamy is the first time in my life that I spent that much time with someone only to emerge with the stark realization that I haven't begun to scratch the surface of my interest in her.

WTF?

It's like I decided I needed some ice, someone gave me Antarctica and I looked at it and said, *Hmm, yeah, but have you got anything bigger?*

I knew the weekend was intense and that I didn't want to go overboard or hit her like a ton of bricks. I knew I needed to play it cool and take a breather. Give *her* a breather.

But I'm telling you…

When that moment came for her to get out of my car and for me to say goodbye to her, even just for the night, I couldn't do it.

That's how I felt. Still feel.

So I was sub-thrilled when she hesitated before smiling at me with unmistakable regret.

"I've got to return to my regularly scheduled life. Get some stuff done around the apartment. And you've had enough of me by now, haven't you?"

No! I haven't!

"Come later, then," I said immediately.

Another hesitation. Another regretful smile.

"Be careful, boss. You don't want your assistant falling in love with you, do you?"

Yes! I do! That sounds like a slice of heaven to me!

Luckily, she leaned in and gave me a tender kiss to cap off the weekend. Then she got out and disappeared into her apartment building, consigning me to a night without her that was every bit as long and miserable as I'd feared it would be. Worse, she left me to realize that we hadn't even discussed how we're going to proceed from now until the end of the summer.

Am I an idiot, or what? And what about—

My phone buzzes next to my legal pad, jarring me out of my thoughts. I stop scribbling, spare a quick glance at the lawyer—Jesus Christ; still droning—and check the display.

It's a headless selfie of a woman showering, with heavy emphasis on her pale breasts, jutting pink nipples and the hand between her legs.

I sigh and give the photo a dispassionate once-over. It's a nice shot and a great body, but only one woman sends me these shower selfies, and it ain't Bellamy.

Sure enough, there's a text to go with it. From Claire, an investment banker I hook up with a couple of times a month or so.

Thinking about you. I'm in the neighborhood. Coffee?

Can't, I type without regret, glad I have a ready excuse. Claire and I have always been heavy on the fucking but light on the talking. Even if I weren't drowning in all things Bellamy right now, grabbing coffee with Claire would be exactly as exciting as the meeting I'm currently suffering through. *Stuck in a meeting.*

She responds immediately.

Alas! Can't wait till Friday night. We still on?

I frown down at my phone. Friday night? Am I forgetting something? And then it hits me. We're supposed to hook up at my place Friday night. We scheduled it a few weeks back because we're always so busy. I promised her lobster and champagne. She promised me Agent Provocateur lingerie and a blow job.

I hesitate, choosing my words carefully.

Sorry. Can't Friday. I was going to text you. Something's come up. Let me get back to you.

I hit send, pleased that I've managed to sound suffi-ciently vague and neutral. Until her response arrives.

Who is she? Her pussy can't be as hot as mine.

Good old Claire. Subtle as always.

Take care of yourself, I tell her, then turn my phone off and wonder how much more suffering I'll have to endure before the morning ends.

Luckily, the meeting seems to be breaking up.

"I'll know more tomorrow after I make some calls," the lawyer says. "I'll keep you posted."

A murmur of relief ripples around the table as we all stand and stretch. The lawyers file out, taking their never-ending opinion letters and memos with them. Damon, meanwhile, wastes no time hurrying over to give me shit.

"If I didn't know any better, I'd say you were looking for someone," he says with that familiar brotherly malice in his eyes. "Coincidentally, I noticed that Bellamy isn't here yet. Missing her, are you?"

"Not sure what you're talking about," I say, willing my cheeks not to burn as I grab my coffee and head for the door. "She'll be here in a minute."

"I'm talking about that shit-eating look on your face," he says with a grin of delight. "Look at you. You look all *happy* and *glowy*. Got you wrapped around that pussy already?"

Yes. Yes, she does.

"Shut the fuck up," I tell Damon with a warning glance at Ryker to make sure *he* doesn't get any cute ideas about joining in the fun. "Watch your mouth about Bellamy."

"Whoa," Damon says. My brothers exchange looks of poorly concealed glee. "This is worse than we thought."

I do my best to puff up and look threatening, but that's tough to do when I'm so happy with the sudden change in my relationship with Bellamy that my feet barely touch the ground now. "You need to knock it off before I—"

One set of elevator doors chooses that exact moment to slide open, and there she is. My girl, wearing a pale green dress that looks as though it was cut specially for her curves. I freeze. Our gazes connect immediately. I'm aware of our avid audience in the form of my two jackass brothers, but I can no more stop my grin from exploding across my face than I can voluntarily elect to stop needing air to live. My only consolation? She seems just as happy to see me.

"You'd better pull it together, Griff," Ryker says, sounding vaguely awed and alarmed as he follows my line of sight and whacks me in the belly with the back of his hand. "She's going to take you out for the count if you're not careful."

Don't I know it?

"You know what's going to happen if *you're* not careful?" I say, never taking my eyes off Bellamy as she walks to her desk and puts her things away. "I'm going to start in on *you*. Start talking shit about you and a certain pastry chef named Ella. How does that sound?"

"Now you're just being nasty."

We all head for the door, still laughing, until another set of elevator doors slides open and ejects Claire, whose sharp eagle eyes immediately register the way I'm grinning at Bellamy (and the way she's once again looking at me as she slides into her chair) before I can whip my smile back into something neutral. I watch as Claire's expression hardens into something that would turn Medusa to stone, my heart sinking.

"Uh-oh," Damon says, taking the words out of my mouth. He's seen Claire once or twice when she's met me here at the office. "Isn't that your little fuck buddy?"

"Yep," I say grimly, picking up my pace and making a mental note to have a word with security downstairs to make sure this never happens again. "Excuse me, guys."

It all unfolds like some twisted nightmare straight out of *The Twilight Zone*. Bellamy's bewildered gaze swings between me and Claire. I see the exact moment the light of comprehension clicks on in her eyes, her smile fades and her face floods with color. To her credit, though, she keeps her professional façade firmly in place even if it is much chillier than it was a second ago.

Shit.

I spent enough time in her doghouse on Saturday night. I have no desire to return there, especially over some Claire bullshit.

"Morning, Bellamy," I say, determined to tread lightly on this cracking ice beneath my feet.

"Boss," she says pleasantly without making eye contact. "Looks like you have a visitor. Let me know if you need me to bump your nine-thirty meeting. I'm getting coffee."

I watch her walk off, my heart sinking even further when I see the rigidity in her spine, then turn to Claire with murder in my heart.

"I could've sworn I said I don't have time to see you today," I tell her.

"Really?" Claire says. "*Her*? I'm disappointed in you, Griffin. I thought you'd be more original than doing your assistant."

"You need to *leave*," I say, barely able to get the words out through my gritted jaw.

"Honestly, Griff, it's okay," she says, edging closer and giving me her sultriest look. "We're both free agents. I'm an adult. I don't care who else you fuck. But don't cancel on me. I've been looking forward to Friday for *weeks*."

Well, there it is. Music to any man's ears. Claire is a

gorgeous blonde with big blue eyes, a smoking-hot body and stellar skills in bed. As recently as a couple of weeks ago, I would've taken her up on her offer without giving it a second thought. But now all I can think about is getting rid of her so I can make sure Bellamy and I are still on track. And when Claire walks out of here, I won't give her a second thought. Just like I haven't thought twice about any of the other women I've been with. A distant part of me wonders if I'd ever be able to dismiss Bellamy from my life this easily, then doubles up and busts a gut laughing.

"Sorry," I tell Claire, making a mental note to block her on my phone as soon as she leaves. "It's over. And I need to get back to work."

I don't know Claire that well, but you don't have to be a genius to recognize the emotions that quickly scroll across her face. Hurt. Anger. Spite.

Lobbing a final scathing look at the dead center of my forehead, she pivots and strides off without a word. I manage half a sigh of relief and gratitude that nothing worse has happened when Bellamy emerges from the kitchen with her coffee. It's just my bad luck that Claire sees her and veers in her direction, making a slight detour on her way to the elevator.

"Enjoy him while you can, sweetie," she tells a startled Bellamy. "Just don't make the mistake of thinking he has more to offer you than a few good orgasms. He's always got someone waiting in the wings to take your place. Take it from me. Have a great day."

With that, Claire glides onto the elevator like the Wicked Witch of the West whizzing off on her broomstick. My last sight of her, hopefully forever, is when the doors close on her triumphant face.

Then she's gone, leaving me to pick up the pieces with Bellamy as best I can.

"Listen…" I begin.

But Bellamy seems determined never to look me in the eye again.

"Don't forget to get me your expenses this morning, boss," she says, brushing by me on her way back to her desk. "And let me know what you want to do about your lunch reservation. Also, if I remember correctly, Claire really liked the gardenias last time. So let me know if I should send those again."

Her aloofness and crisp tone push all my buttons in the worst possible way. Which is surely her goal.

"I'm not sending her any fucking flowers. And don't call me *boss*."

"Just trying to do my job." She sets her coffee on her desk with a loud and defiant thunk. *"Boss."*

"We need to talk about this," I say, keeping my voice low. I'm acutely aware that we're in a semi-public place and could be interrupted at any second. "Let's go in my office."

"I've got a lot of work to do," she says, sitting and swiveling to face her computer.

With that, I've maxed out on my patience. She's picked the wrong fight if she wants to see who's the biggest asshole around here. They don't call me the Beast for nothing.

"My office, Forest. *Now*," I bark.

She hesitates, finally meets my gaze and shoots laser strikes from her eyes that are strong enough to smoke my eyebrows and set off the overhead sprinklers. Then she stiffly stands and marches past me into my office. I slam the door behind us.

Alone at last. I feel a tremendous surge of satisfaction. Time for us to get a few things straight.

"Something on your mind, Bellamy?" I make a sweeping gesture as I go stand behind my desk. "The floor is yours."

"There's no point," she says, shrugging. "I'd be foolish to get upset with you for being who you are. Who you always were. Besides. It's not like we're in a real relationship."

I recoil as though she's taken a Taser and zapped me in the neck with it. Disbelieving, I rest my hands on my desk and lean into it.

"Excuse me?" I ask quietly. "What was that whole big scene about on Saturday night if we're not in a *real relationship*?"

"I mean…" She hesitates, her defiance wobbling. "We like to sleep together. Obviously. And I don't like it when you act like we can't get to know each other better. But we never said—"

"You know what?" I say, straightening. "You're absolutely right. There's a bunch of stuff I need to say. Have a seat."

"I don't want—"

"Sit your ass down, Bellamy," I say, exasperated. "Give me a break. For *once*."

She blinks. Plops down. Crosses her legs. Waits.

"I'm no expert, but I thought a *real relationship* was that thing where you *think* about the person"—I tap my temple—"all the time. *All the time*. Where you don't want to see anyone else because your head is so full of wondering how the person is doing and what the person is thinking about and when you'll see the person again that there's no room for anyone else. Am I crazy? Do I need to check my definitions here?"

"Griffin…" she says, softening.

"I want you. I *only* want you." My cheeks, ears and throat are seriously burning now, making the words hard to get out. To say nothing of my hoarse voice. "I don't want to see anyone else. I sure as shit don't want *you* to see anyone else. That's where I'm at. Also? That whole thing last night where you sent me on my merry way by myself and didn't invite me to stay with you? That doesn't work for me. You're not going to be here that much longer. I don't plan to waste the little time we have. I don't care where we spent our nights. As long as we spend them together. So unless I hear an objection in the next ten seconds, that's what we're going to do."

She opens her mouth.

"You'd better not be about to object," I quickly tell her. "Swear to God."

She snaps her mouth closed again, treating me to a luminous smile instead. Everything inside me stands down and catches its breath.

Funny how I'm the wealthier person here. The owner. The boss. The physically larger person. The older and ostensibly wiser person. The person with the most dating experience.

Yet this woman has a terrifying and absolute power over me. And she doesn't even know it.

"Am I allowed to speak now?" she asks, a spark of amusement in her eyes.

"If you choose your words wisely, sure."

I'm absolutely riveted and paralyzed by what she might say next. No joke.

"Can I get back to work now? Now that that's settled? I have a very demanding boss."

I manage an offhand shrug. "Suit yourself," I say, all but sagging with relief.

A crisp nod from Bellamy. She heads for the door, leaving me to collapse in my chair, rest my elbows on my desk and press my face to my hands while I get my heartbeat regulated.

This is *exactly* why I never let people in if I can help it. It takes too damn much out of me.

I can't see what's going on, but I hear the quiet swish of her dress as she comes around to my side of the desk. The next thing I know, she puts a hand on my neck and curls her fingers into the hair at my nape.

This unexpected tenderness is more than I can take right now. Making a crazy strangled sound, I swivel my chair, wrap my arms tight around her waist and press my face to the fragrant valley between her breasts so I can gratefully breathe in her scent of roses and reset my mood now that all is right with my world again.

This whole thing is crazy. I know that. But I'm seriously beginning to wonder how I cobbled together an existence without her in my life exactly like *this*.

As for the question of what kind of existence I'll have when she leaves? I can't even go there.

Speaking of not going there…

The familiar need starts to bubble inside me. I remind myself that we're at work and loosen my grip on her enough to push her back and look up into her face. It's gratifying to see the rising color in her cheeks and the sultry light in her eyes.

"Your place or mine tonight?" I ask her.

"Yours."

"Great. I'll give you my extra key. Fair warning, though. I only bothered with the bare minimum furniture, since I'm never there."

"Noted."

"You go home. Grab some stuff. I'll meet you there after work. I'll get there as soon as I can."

"Okay," she says, looking pleased but stunned.

But not half as stunned as I am. I just promised to give the woman I'm dating a key to my apartment. And I don't regret it. At all. And speaking of stunned, I repress a laugh at the thought of what Claire would say if she were here now.

"Don't steal anything," I warn Bellamy.

"I won't," she says, laughing.

This is a lie, I decide as I watch her go back to work.

She's already well on her way to stealing my heart.

Not that I have a real heart that anyone would want.

13

BELLAMY

"TREATS?" I squeal, clapping as I swing my apartment door open for Ella early one evening a couple of days later. After work, I raced home, showered and slipped into a cute gold sundress in eager anticipation of Griffin's imminent arrival. I'd planned to spend some time looking over some of my printouts of available apartments at Berkeley, or maybe reading more of *Pride and Prejudice* (Griffin let me borrow it from his library), but that can wait. I'm never too busy to receive guests bearing food. "For me?"

"Yes, yes, try to contain yourself," Ella says, laughing and balancing a platter of beautiful petit fours as she comes inside and heads for my kitchen. Being best friends with a pastry chef who lives in my building is the best thing that ever happened to my sweet tooth and the worst thing that ever happened to my waistline. She's a bit too generous about sharing all her new recipes, and I'm a bit too enthusiastic in my role as guinea pig. "There's plenty to go around."

"Another round of rejects? Too much almond flavoring again?"

"Not exactly," she says, leading the way to my kitchen table, which is small like everything else in my one-bedroom apartment, where she sits. "The mom who placed the order decided that she wanted sparkly shoes instead of sparkly crowns on her little princess's first birthday party treats, so she changed her order."

"It's hard out there for an Upper East Side princess these days," I say, abandoning my plans to order pizza and reaching for plates, napkins and a bottle of Prosecco I keep for just such occasions instead. "Great news for me, though."

"Indeed. Are you going to do anything about that yapping in the bedroom?"

I sigh. While other people have lovely golden retrievers who love everybody and make lifelong friends wherever they go, well-trained and clever German shepherds that protect them from harm or even cute little purse dogs, I have Jeremy the Ill-Mannered. Who has never, to my knowledge, shown one ounce of gratitude to me or my friends for rescuing his furry little ass two years ago.

"I wanted to give you a minute to come in and catch your breath first. Are you ready for him?"

"As I'll ever be," Ella says with mock cheer.

Girding my loins, I open my bedroom door and release the Tasmanian devil of dogs. Out races Jeremy, barking his fool head off. He makes a beeline for Ella, dancing and snarling at her feet as though he's Floyd Mayweather rather than a ten-pound and sandy-colored version of Toto.

"It's me, Jeremy," she says wearily, holding out a

hand for him to sniff and hopefully remember that she's a friend and not a foe. "Why do we have to go through this every single time? You *know* me. I give you treats."

This makes no difference to Jeremy the Ungrateful, who continues to snarl until I hand Ella a treat to give him. He crunches it down, then immediately stops barking, stands on his hind legs and puts his paws on Ella's knees for her to pick him up, a loving and conciliatory gesture that fools no one.

Ella purses her lips, shakes her head and drapes him across her lap, a perch that allows him to oversee everything with bright interest.

We settle in happily, distributing petit fours and popping the cork.

"Here's to your new man," I say, raising my glass to Ella.

"I don't have a new man," she says, working hard to repress a sheepish smile as she scratches Jeremy's ears. "Here's to *your* new man."

"*I* don't have a new man either."

We clink glasses and burst into laughter.

"Your skin looks bright and healthy. I know what *that* means," I say, then dig into my petit four with gusto.

"Oh, no you don't. You go first. How go things with the Beast?"

"Stop calling him that. He doesn't deserve it. I wish I'd never given him that nickname," I say, regretting my snappish tone as soon as the words come out of my mouth.

Ironic, I know. *I'm* the one who christened him with the nickname in the first place. But I'm feeling surprisingly protective toward him lately, and that unexpectedly tender interlude in his office this morning has only heightened the sensation. Not that I plan to let Ella know about my growing weakness for him. That way lies disaster.

But…too late.

"Oh my God." Her eyes widen with an unsettling combination of concern and growing horror. "What's going on?"

The look on her face does nothing to settle my nerves, which are already rattled by the speed and intensity with which things are developing between me and Griffin. Is this an ideal time for me to fall for someone? No. Is he an ideal candidate for anyone's Prince Charming? God, no. But let's keep things in perspective. It's not as though I showed up at a family dinner and introduced Ted Bundy as my date.

"Nothing," I say, reaching for my glass and then taking a gulp or two because it gives me an excuse not to look in her face while I manufacture one lie after another. I'm not sure whether it's more important for me to convince her or myself. "We had fun in the Hamptons. Things were a little strange at work the other day, but we got through it. He'll be here in a minute. That's all there is to it."

I try an offhand shrug, but it feels awkward, as though I'm working the shoulders on someone else's body.

"Bellamy. This is supposed to be just sex at most. No feelings. A summer fling only. We talked about this."

"I know. I'm *fine*."

Ella gives me a skeptical look. "So…this is strictly sex? Is that what you're telling me?"

"We haven't exactly labeled it," I say, deciding that now's not the time to mention, say, our little emotional breakthrough on Saturday night or my bout of jealousy and his reassurance at the office. "We're just enjoying each other for now. No big deal."

"No big deal until he moves on to his next flavor of the month and I have to talk you down from the ledge," she says darkly. "You've had a crush on him this whole time. I thought you'd hook up with him once or twice. I don't like this whole"—she swirls a hand to encompass my entire body—"attachment vibe I'm getting from you."

"I'm not *attached*," I say, but my voice sounds high and squeaky.

"Do *not* fall in love with him, Bellamy," she says with the exact urgency you'd expect someone to say, *Do not step in the quicksand!* or *Do not keep driving on this flooded road!* "This is not the guy for you. On top of you leaving soon, and him being your boss and a player, he's also a jerk ninety-five percent of the time. Don't forget that. I'm sure he's nice now that he's getting laid on the regular, but don't expect him to have a personality transplant."

"I *don't*," I say, but she's right and I know it.

I *am* falling in love with him even though I'm about to move across the country. He *is* my boss, a player and a jerk.

This breezy summer affair is going to end badly for me. Only two questions remain:

How badly? and

Which of those poison pills are going to do it in?

And yet…

"He's not all bad," I say, as much to myself as to Ella.

"I'm sure his dick is *great*."

"I could do without the sarcasm," I say, scowling. "I just mean that…there's more to him. There's a lot more to him than I ever expected."

Right on cue, someone knocks.

"Speak of the devil," I say as Jeremy leaps off her lap and races to the door to commence another round of yapping. "I told the doorman to let him up."

"This should be interesting," she says, also standing.

I quickly scoop Jeremy up, toss him back into the bedroom and shut the door. No need for Griffin to be assaulted by my best friend *and* my dog at the same time.

"Hey," I say, blushing furiously as I let Griffin in. I'm far too grateful and eager to see him again for someone who last saw him two hours ago at work. There's no way I can hide it. "You made it."

He's still wearing his suit, but the first couple of buttons of his shirt are undone now, and his tie is gone. Also gone? His office demeanor and expression. Instead, his face and smile are purest sunshine, as though he's been possessed by the spirit of a kid who just received a free trip to Disney World for his birthday.

I swear to God, that smile touches my soul.

"I made it," he says as he unslings his crossbody bag from his shoulder and leans it against the wall, and there's such a contrast between this soft voice that he uses just for me and his booming office voice that I can't help but feel stunned as we reach for each other.

I'm not sure what he has in mind as he pulls me in and I wrap my arms around his neck. I wouldn't cry if he wanted to take me hard and fast up against the nearest wall, but poor Ella might never recover. I open my mouth to mention that we're not alone, but it's not neces- sary. He wraps his arms tight around me and uses one hand to anchor the back of my head as he presses a kiss to my cheek.

A shudder ripples through his body as we sway together with me on my tiptoes.

"Now I can breathe again," he says quietly. "Now I can *breathe*."

I would've been happy to let this continue forever, but he suddenly stiffens.

"Hi," he says, turning me loose and extending a hand to Ella. "Didn't see you. Griffin Black."

"I know," she says, eyes bright with amusement as she and Griffin shake. "Ella Richardson. We've met several times when I came to the office to meet Bellamy for lunch. You've grunted and/or glared at me a good five or six times over the last year or so."

"Sorry about that." He ducks his head and rubs the back of his neck, a dull flush climbing over his cheeks. "I'm beginning to see why Bellamy nicknamed me the Beast."

"It's well earned," says Ella, who never misses a chance to rake someone over the coals if she can help it. "I didn't even know you could smile."

"Neither did I," he says with a sidelong glance at me, dimples deepening.

"I've decided I don't hate you," Ella says with a nod. "You may have a petit four."

"Thanks," he says, looking relieved. "I take that as a ringing endorsement. By the way, you know who else is doing a lot of smiling these days?"

"I can't imagine," Ella says lightly as she tucks her hair behind her ear, but she's no Diane Keaton and she can't *quite* lock down her simper.

"My brother," he says, clearly relishing this quick turning of the tables. "My brother *Ryker*. In case there's any confusion."

"My goodness, would you look at the time," she says with an exaggerated look at her watch-free wrist. "Why didn't you tell me it was so late, Bellamy? Now I'm going to have to dash off without finishing this important conversation."

We all laugh.

Ella turns to me. "More to him, eh?" she asks.

"More to him," I say, grateful that she's seeing this other side of him and hopefully doesn't think I'm completely insane.

"More to *who*?" he asks. I can feel his keen interest sharpening.

"No one you know," Ella and I say together.

There's another round of laughter, then Ella edges toward the door.

"I really should go. I've got another batch of petit fours in the oven. Great seeing you, Griffin."

"Stick around. I was just about to take Bellamy to dinner. Why don't you come?"

Ella looks startled and touched by this suggestion. As I am.

"Thanks. Another time," she tells him. "You kids have fun."

"I'll text you later," I tell her as she lets herself out.

"That was very nice of you," I tell him when the door shuts behind her.

"I'm a very nice guy. Ask anyone. Stop laughing. Is it my imagination, or is some crazy dog barking in your apartment?"

"That is definitely not your imagination," I say glumly. "That's Jeremy. Who embarrasses me every chance he gets."

"Well, let him out. Let's meet him."

"Foolish words," I mutter.

"Let's go. I love dogs."

"You say that now…"

I repeat the drill, opening the bedroom door for Jeremy. Jeremy races out, barking his fool head off.

Until Griffin takes a step in his direction and stops him cold, mid-bark.

"Relax, Jeremy," he says in a soothing but commanding voice that reveals he has some significant Dog Whisperer blood running through his veins. "Stop all the commotion."

I watch in utter disbelief as Jeremy whines and backs up a few steps.

Griffin squats and snaps his fingers. "Get over here."

Jeremy the Rotten zooms over, tail wagging, and wriggles happily as Griffin scoops him up in a football hold. A canine groan of ecstasy makes me wonder if Jeremy will be packing his little bags and heading home with Griffin when he leaves. Griffin raises a brow and gives me a smug look, apparently amused by my drop-jawed amazement. If he knows or cares about the dog hair he's probably getting on his dark custom suit, he doesn't show it.

"Anyone else around here that I need to charm?"

"No," I say sourly, waving him to the sofa. "You've done quite enough already."

Still chuckling, he sits and arranges the dog across his lap. "So this is the place, eh?"

"This is the place. I'm going to give you the nickel tour. Which will be nothing like the nickel tour you gave me of your house in the Hamptons, trust me. So don't blink or you'll miss everything."

"Got it."

"Living room. Kitchen. Bedroom. Bathroom. That's it. I like to think of it as ten square feet of paradise."

He takes it all in, nodding. "What do they call this? Shabby chic?"

"Exactly."

"Love it. Love all the neutrals. Very warm and cozy. Very *you*."

"Thanks." To hide my ridiculous flush of pleasure at this praise, I head to the kitchen. "Prosecco? I just opened a bottle."

"Sure."

"Help yourself to a petit four if you want one. Ella's a great pastry chef. But don't try to sneak any treats to Jeremy when I'm not looking. And don't fall for his sad face. He's playing you."

I return to the living room, glasses in hand, to find him shifting my Berkeley apartment listings on the coffee table, frowning.

"What's wrong?" I say.

"What the fuck is all this?" he demands, glaring up at me.

14

GRIFFIN

THERE I GO, lapsing into dickhead mode again. It's a real talent. If I have any doubts about how abrasive I just managed to sound, Bellamy's startled expression immediately removes them. Hell, even the dog is looking up at me, a perplexed look on his furry face.

Yet I plow ahead like a rodeo bull turned loose in the fine china and crystal department at Macy's, destroying the peace in my determination to get the answers I need from Bellamy.

"You're looking for an apartment in Berkeley? Already?" I've barely had the chance to enjoy *this* apartment, which is so much warmer and cozier than my apartment. *That* place has stellar views of the city, true, but with its sad lack of furniture and echoing emptiness, it feels like an airplane hangar. "I thought you weren't moving until August."

"I'm not," she says, passing me my glass of Prosecco as she sits in the chair to my right. She seems neutral now. "But that's not much time for me to find a new place. Which you should know, since you're in real estate. I'm starting to look. I'll probably make a weekend trip or two out there to see what I can find."

A weekend trip *or two* — ?

The hits just keep on coming. As if I haven't got my hands full trying not to lose my shit over her pending departure, now I have to worry about these weekend trips cutting into our already limited time together. Why can't we just enjoy each other for two seconds without these constant reminders that it can't last?

"I'll go with you. Help you find something," I say.

"Really?"

I don't know why she looks so surprised. She should know by now that I'll do anything to keep that exact look of delight on her face. Discover the lost city of Atlantis? Buy her a private island? Done.

"Of course," I say. "Just say when."

"Thank you." She presses a hand to her heart. "I appreciate the help. I've got so many things to do before I leave. And I'm feeling so unsettled now that I've let my apartment go. It's like I don't belong anywhere right now."

Keeping my mouth shut and not spouting nonsense — *You belong with me* quickly comes to mind — takes every ounce of my energy.

"Will you have to vacate this apartment before school starts?"

"No. Luckily."

I don't feel so lucky that I won't have the opportunity to suggest she move in with me for the rest of the summer, but I decide to keep that to myself as well.

"Right," I say, absently stroking the dog's head. A sip or two of the Prosecco and Bellamy's calming presence start to mellow me out a bit, especially when she slips over to the sofa and sits beside me.

"Hey," she says, leaning in for a kiss.

"Hey."

I keep it short and sweet, emerging glazed with pleasure but not quite ready to rip her clothes off just yet. I want to wallow in her space for a minute. Her sofa. Her dog's comforting presence on my lap. Her romance books and linen-scented candle on the mantel. The crystalline sparkle of her brown eyes and the steady warmth of her smile she looks at me.

"Thanks for the invite," I say, savoring the moment even more because it spares me from another night alone in the echoing emptiness of my apartment. "I'm glad to be here."

"Good."

I'm about to dive back in—another kiss never hurt anyone—when she pulls back, snapping her fingers.

"That reminds me. I didn't get the chance to mention it before I came home, but I've lined up several great candidates for us to interview to replace me."

I blink, my growing sensual haze making me slow to shift gears. *What?*

"My replacement," she says, now riffling through her papers on the coffee table. "I have some of the résumés right here, if you want to take a look."

See? There it is again.

I'm leaving you, Griffin. Don't get too used to me because I'm not sticking around. Matter of fact, I can't enjoy our time together because I'm so consumed with planning my departure.

"I don't want to take a look," I say. "What part of this aren't you getting? I'm trying to relax. I don't want to talk about you leaving. I don't want to talk about work.

Work belongs at the office. It doesn't belong here on the sofa in between us."

"A thousand pardons, boss," she says acidly.

My entire body stiffens. So much for mellowing out. "Don't call me *boss*."

"If you start acting like the Beast, I'm calling you *boss*. I don't care where we are." Her eyes are flinty chips of amber now, making me marvel at my ability to piss her off this quickly and thoroughly. "I don't want to leave you in the lurch when I move. That's all. I think we should hire a new person as soon as possible so I can get them trained before I go. I'm doing everything I can to make this transition as smooth as possible for you."

I bite back a bitter burst of laughter.

Is she for real? The simplest and easiest thing she could do for me would be to stay here. Where it feels like she's auditioning to be the center of my universe.

But I can't say that. I can never say that. I may be a jackass, but I'm not a selfish jackass. Going to Berkeley Law is Bellamy's lifelong dream. And seeing Bellamy happily reach her highest potential is *my* dream. I'm not sure when or how that happened or why I feel such a pressing urgency about it, but it did. I do. That being the case, I need to keep my big mouth shut and get my shit together. ASAP.

"I appreciate your consideration," I say, taking great care to soften my tone. "But work stays at work from now on. Period."

"I appreciate your desire to separate work time and private time," she says with an edge in her voice that could cut diamonds.

"Okay…?" I say warily.

"You know what *I'd* appreciate? You not firing orders

at me like you're a drill sergeant and I'm a marine in basic training. At work *or* at home." She pauses to flash me a chilling smile. "Agreed?"

"Agreed," I say quickly, probably because the memory of my brief but painful interlude in her doghouse Saturday night is still fresh. If she brought me to heel that easily on *my* turf, I don't want to find out what she could do to me on hers. "Are you done giving me grief?"

"For now," she says, then her triumphant smile disappears behind her glass as she takes a sip.

"Great." I set my glass down, scoot the dog off my lap and stand, determined to, I don't know, take a minute, get my head together and regroup. I can't continue to lose my cool every time things don't go my way with Bellamy. Which, let's face it, is most of the time. "I'll be right back."

"Down the hall. First door," she says.

I retreat to the bathroom, splash water on my face and stare at the poor bastard in the mirror. Funny how I look the same on the outside (except for a veiled flare of panic if you look deep enough into my eyes), yet my insides feel as though they're being remodeled into something for which I haven't seen the floor plan. She's got me tied up in knots, this one.

Part of me thinks I should anticipate the day she leaves as the day I get my normal life back.

A bigger and smarter part of me knows that ain't happening.

I open the door and head toward the living room just as her phone rings.

"Hey, Papa," she says. "Everything okay? It's not really a good time for me to talk."

Her *father*. I linger in the doorway, overcome by sudden overwhelming curiosity.

"Fine, fine," he says. "Just call me tomorrow when you get a chance. Nothing's going on here—"

"Is that your father?" I say quickly, walking in, resuming my seat and crowding her in my attempt to see the screen.

Let me pause here to mention that I don't do parents. If I find myself meeting the parents of a woman I'm sleeping with, something has gone badly wrong with my day. Which is why I find my sudden impulsivity so inexplicable.

My only defense? The devil made me do it.

"Griffin Black," I tell him, settling Jeremy back on my lap when he climbs on board and doing my best to ignore both Bellamy's outraged gasp and sidelong glare. "Great to finally meet you. Bellamy talks about you all the time."

"So *this* is the famous Griffin Black," he says, smiling out at me from the phone. I like him right away. He's got white hair and an open and easy vibe, like a surfer Santa Claus. "You don't look half as bad as Bellamy claims."

"I'm probably much worse. And thanks for the tip about my roses," I say, laughing and ignoring an additional disgruntled sound from Bellamy, this one accompanied by a swift kick to my shin. "Hopefully, we can keep them from dying."

"Let me know if there's anything I can do," he says. "Roses can be finicky. Didn't know that was *your* beautiful garden. Or that your boss was your new boyfriend, Bellamy. That's why you've been so smiley lately."

Smiley? Really?

I pivot at the waist, eager to see Bellamy's reaction to her father's assessment.

"He's not my boyfriend," she says quickly, her smile turning brittle around the edges as her face floods with color. "We're just getting to know each other. A little. It's all very, ah, casual. And I'm leaving soon anyway, so…"

"As long as he knows you're not afraid of a good sexual harassment lawsuit if he doesn't treat you right," he says, and there's that booming and good-natured laugh again. "I'm keeping my eye on you, Griffin."

"I wouldn't expect anything else," I say, stung more than I'd like to admit by Bellamy's vehement disclaimer. But I'll circle back to that in a minute. "When are you coming east? The three of us can grab dinner."

This seems to be a bridge too far for Bellamy.

"We need to let you go, Daddy," she says hastily before he can respond to my invitation. "We don't want to be late for our dinner reservation. Love you. Bye."

She hangs up, tosses the phone aside and looks at me as though I've grown three new heads.

"What the hell?" she cries. "What was *that*?"

I twitch my shoulders in an irritable shrug. "I wanted to meet your father."

"Why?"

"Why?" I echo blankly.

"Yes, *why*?"

Good question, genius. Give it your best shot coming up with an answer.

"I want to know more about you," I say.

She presses a hand to her neck, clutching mock pearls. "Careful. You're getting dangerously close to crossing a line."

"*Your* flagrant line crossing started us down this road in the first place, didn't it?"

She frowns. "Are you complaining?"

"Not at all," I say, giving her an appreciative once-over that lingers on a few pertinent body parts.

The air shifts in the room.

We regard each other warily for a beat or two, like opponents entering a ring and circling each other just as the bell rings for round one.

I don't want to come on like a sledgehammer, but subtlety is not a skill I seem to possess right now. Or at all when it comes to her.

"Not your boyfriend, huh? *That* seems like a firm line," I say, categorically unable to keep the bite out of my voice.

"It's a big word," she says on a laugh that has more than a tinge of awkwardness in it. "I would never presume to—"

"What was the point of our discussion at the office the other day?" I ask. "I thought we'd settled this. What's the term for when you start fucking someone you've known well for a year and you're crazy about them? *Special friend*? *Companion*?"

"*You're* asking *me*?" She can barely contain her outrage. "*You're* the one who freaked out when I tried to get too close the other night and ask about your mother. And now you think I'm going to throw around a label like *boyfriend*? Why would I do that unless I wanted to drive you away forever? Why do we need labels anyway? What is this? Seventh grade? What's gotten into you?"

Like I know. Maybe I need to check in with the scientific community. See if there's a word for when someone sneaks under your skin and into your bloodstream when you least expect it, commandeering your every thought, breath and heartbeat like some emotional virus.

Am I being illogical and absurd? Sure. I'll cop to that.

But I need some official standing in her life. It feels important that we both understand that what the two of us have isn't the same old, same old.

If only I possessed the words and the composure to explain that to her.

But I can't. It's locked up too deep inside me.

"Nothing," I say instead. "Forget I said anything. Are we grabbing dinner or not? We have reservations and this conversation is going nowhere, so…"

She winces as though I've suggested a quick dinner on the rim of an erupting volcano. "You know what? Let's just order a pizza. It's been a long day and I think we're both tired. I'm not looking forward to you glaring across the table at me for two hours."

Right. Why would she agree about dinner when we can't agree about anything else? Why would she be excited that I went to the trouble to plan a lovely evening for her at this great new restaurant in Tribeca? Why can't I get a bead on where this woman's head is at any given moment? Most importantly, why can't I control my temper for two consecutive seconds? It would sure make my life easier.

"Fine," I say, grateful she's not canceling the evening altogether.

"Great," she says, reaching for her bag.

Meanwhile, I reach for my phone to cancel the reservation. By the time I tune back into what *she's* doing, she's got her phone in one hand and her credit card in the other.

It takes me a minute to get over the incongruity of what I'm seeing.

I've got a net worth of a Jay-Z or several Justin Biebers, but she thinks I'm letting *her* pay for dinner?

The fuck—?

"What're you doing?" I demand.

"Ordering dinner," she says, looking startled.

"Put your card away. I'll get it."

"I can afford dinner, Griffin," she says, her volume cranking steadily higher.

As if that's the point. As if I'm the sort of man who'd let her spend one penny on me when she's about to spend three years as a student with probably little to no income and will need every dime she's got.

"I'm not letting you pay for dinner. Or anything. Ever. So move on."

"Oh my God," she says, hanging up and tossing the phone aside. "Do you even hear yourself? *Letting me*? I'm a grown woman. I do what I want. Especially in my own damn apartment."

"Calm down. Stop overreacting."

In the ringing silence that follows, it occurs to me that I've veered deep into dangerous territory and may need a rescue party to get myself out. Even the dog, no doubt sensing the brewing storm, hops down from my lap, gives me a sad *You're on your own now, buddy* backward glance and retreats to his bed over in the corner.

Leaving me to face Bellamy's growing wrath by myself.

Since I can see the slow curl of steam coming out of

her ears and her kitchen knives are within easy reach, a little back-pedaling seems appropriate.

"I didn't mean—"

She gets up and gestures toward the door. "I think we should finish the rest of this conversation at the office tomorrow. Since you seem so determined to bark out orders and bully me. *Boss*."

Her unrestrained use of the B-word at this tense moment scrapes over my nerves like using a wire grill-cleaning brush to scratch my sunburned back. Do I have some rough edges? Yeah. But I'm not that monstrous *other* that everyone always makes me out to be. And I'm trying here. I am *trying*.

I stand too, the better to look her in the eye so she can see how serious I am about this one point.

"Don't call me *boss*."

She takes an aggressive step forward, puts her hands on her hips and hikes up her chin as though she plans to take a swing at me. I watch her, as fascinated as I am infuriated. Has she secretly been like this the whole time I've known her? How did she suddenly become so effective at pushing my buttons?

"If you don't like the nickname, then *stop earning it*. You're not in charge here."

Ain't that the fucking truth?

Once upon a time, I was the king of my world. Now I'm just a puppet dancing at the end of her strings while praying my choreography pleases her enough to keep me around for a little while longer.

I think about all the things I'm no longer in charge of. My thoughts. My hormones. My emotions.

The bottom line? She's right. One hundred percent.

I tell you, boy, of all the galling things she might have said to me in that moment, she hit the mother lode.

And I absolutely cannot get enough of her. Not that I plan to clue her in on that crucial fact or let her have the last word.

Besides. I can think of one area where I'm quite effective.

"I'm not in charge here?" I ease forward, letting my attention drift to her lips. The silly buttons marching down the front of her little sundress. The slit in the side. "You sure about that?"

She backs up with a flare of alarm.

Not *alarm* alarm.

Sensual alarm.

"Don't look at me like that," she says, color rising up her neck and flooding her cheeks as her voice turns husky and her breath hitches. And I can suddenly see the prominent beads of her nipples, plain as the nose on my face. "We're in the middle of an argument because you don't know how to treat people."

"We *were*." I grab her dress's belt and pull her in, ignoring her startled gasp. "Now we're figuring out *who's* in charge of *what*."

15

BELLAMY

LOOK. I wasn't born yesterday. I know he's trying to handle me. I know that Griffin and I spend as much time battling each other and jockeying for position as we do having sex. We're like Romeo and Juliet locked in some high-stakes chess match. I want to get closer to him emotionally. He wants to block me. He tries to run roughshod over me and everyone else at the office. I block *him* whenever I can. That's how we are together. That's our dynamic. Right now? He wants to boss me around in my own apartment. To have the last word. To dominate me. This latest argument is about money, but it's not about money at all. It's about whether we can ever be equal partners or not. It's about who's in charge. Who's being managed with sex and diversions and who's going to manage.

Who's going to *win*.

I cannot let this arrogant bully win on my turf. I don't care how sexy he is. I'm fighting for the dignity and power of my entire gender right now. Women everywhere are depending on me.

Ten seconds ago, my plan was to shut him down and kick him out if necessary. Simple.

But that was before he laid his hands on me and looked at me with all that smoldering heat and all those dark intentions. Before he set his mind to turning my own weak body against me.

I don't know why everything has to be such a test with him. I just know that I can't fail.

I stand my ground and smack his hands away.

"Get your hands off me."

Crooked smile from Griffin. Wicked smile. Infuriating smile.

"Whatever you say."

He makes a show of holding his hands up as though he's the unfortunate victim of a stick-up. I start to breathe easier. I'm *that* foolish. I actually start to think I've won this round.

Until he takes those same hands, grabs his collar on each side and rips his starched white dress shirt apart right down the middle, sending buttons flying and skittering across my floor. I watch with absolute astonishment as he yanks it off and tosses it aside. His undershirt quickly follows, basically rubbing my face in all those heart-stopping muscles and all that gleaming golden skin. Paralysis sets in until I can't breathe. The ripples of desire inside me become a tidal wave, sweeping away the little bit of air left in my lungs. But the sight of him starting to undo his belt and thereby highlighting the size of his straining erection galvanizes me into action.

"Okay. We're done." I somehow escape the gravitational pull of his body and walk to the door. My voice sounds a little shaky, but hey, I'm doing the best I can here. "This is me calling it a night."

That smile blossoms into a laugh as he makes his way over, taking all the time in the world. A *laugh*.

"We both know you don't want me to leave."

Sadly true, not that I plan to admit it.

"Bye," I say, swinging the door open for him.

He yanks it out of my hand and slams it shut again just as quickly. I turn to face him, determined not to back down now that I'm cornered. I have the vague idea of, I don't know, pushing him away. Not that I'm either physically afraid of him or have the slightest hope of budging him when he doesn't want to be budged. I just have to do *something*. But he plants his hands on both sides of my head, effectively caging me against the door. I take a deep breath and try to steady my nerves. But the gleam of triumph in his eyes—not to mention the flaming heat from his body and the fact that he's right in my face, well within kissing range—sure don't make it easy on a girl.

"Okay. I'll bite." It's a wonder my voice is audible over my galloping heartbeat. "What exactly is it that you want here?"

"That seems obvious. I want to fuck you."

"Hmm. I noticed." I reach between us and give that hard dick of his an appreciative squeeze to knock the smug look off his face. To my immense satisfaction, he tenses and his breath catches. "But now doesn't seem like the best time for that. We were in the middle of an important conversation."

"What can I say? I got distracted."

"Yeah? Well, I'm not in the mood. How about that?"

Another one of those lopsided smiles. "I feel confident I can change your mind."

To prove his point, he runs his lips and nose up the side of my neck and stops at my ear. Nerve endings erupt to life all over my body, and a good fifty percent of the bones in my legs begin to melt. The only thing I can say in my defense is that I catch myself melting and recover enough to shove his shoulders. Hard.

"I told you not to touch me."

"Yeah, but why fight? We both want the same thing."

"The same thing?" I laugh, incredulous. "I don't think we do. *You* want to control me and control how much you let me in. *I* want a real relationship."

The only sign that I've hit a nerve is the telltale pulsing of a muscle in his jaw.

"So now you're a shrink?"

"No. But I don't have to be a shrink to recognize a scared bully when I see one, do I?" I say. "And you're putting a lot of effort into not finishing our conversation."

He goes still, creating a pause long enough for me to wonder if I've gone too far by invoking the SB term.

But I don't regret it. I don't regret it at all.

Until he exacts his revenge.

In one smooth movement, he hooks an arm around my torso, trapping both my arms at my sides in the process, hefts me off my feet and swings me around. Toward the bedroom.

"What are you doing?" I shout, rising frustration making me shrill as I kick my legs and squirm in a useless attempt to escape. It's hard to claim the upper hand in an argument when you're being slung around like a sack of potatoes, but I give it everything I've got. Unfortunately, his unyielding arm is like one of Harry Houdini's straitjackets. "You can't just use sex to shut me up."

"Sure I can."

"*Stop*, Griffin—"

"Not a chance. You want to toss around words like *bully* and *beast*? Let's see how big a beast I can be."

I catch a glimpse of Jeremy, who's drowsily stretched out on his bed with his head resting on his crossed paws.

"Don't just sit there, you dumb dog!" I yell. "Do something! Bite his ankles! Help Mommy!"

Jeremy yawns, unfurling his long pink tongue. That's the last thing I see before Griffin turns into my bathroom, kicks the door shut, sets me on my feet and clicks on the light.

I turn quickly, spitting nails at being manhandled in my own apartment and ready to smack him.

He never gives me the chance.

He's all over me, taking my head in his hands and tilting it way back to give him complete access to my mouth. He takes shameless advantage, laying a kiss on me that's so hard, deep and hot that it's a wonder my entire body doesn't spontaneously combust. And that's all it takes. Oh, sure, I talk a good game about not wanting him to control me. I can act like the standard bearer for empowered women all day long. But way down deep, in the dark places where it really counts, the thing I really want is to be sexually dominated by a partner who knows what he's doing with his mouth, hands and dick.

Exactly like *this*.

Honestly, it's a massive relief to surrender. To wrap my arms around his neck and arch into him so that my aching breasts can find the relief they crave against his hard chest. To hook a leg around his waist to urge him closer. To palm his flexing ass and grind against him as all the blood in my body pools between my thighs. To hiss a helpless *yes* when he finally lets me up for air.

He plants his hands on my hips and lifts me up. Plunks me onto the counter. Wastes no time reaching under my skirt, giving me a hard and determined stare the entire time. Rips my lace bikinis off my body with a loud tear and tosses them to the floor.

"You like this?" he says, unsmiling, as he undoes his belt and jerks his zipper down, revealing the bulge hidden by his gray boxer briefs. "Making me crazy?"

I can't help but laugh. That's the stupidest question God ever allowed anyone to ask.

"What do you think?"

Wrong thing to say.

"I'll tell you what I think." His husky voice acquires a hard edge as his attention dips to my cleavage. "I think you crossed that line between us when I was doing the right thing and minding my own business. I never would have touched you. But now here we are, and you keep spouting bullshit about wanting to get to know me better and wanting a *real relationship*. But you don't want to know the real me. You won't like it."

Does he expect me to back down? To run for cover? He'd better think again.

"Try me."

"Why do we have to get into this?" He sweeps his arms wide. "It should be obvious to you what I'm good for. You want me to spell it out for you? I'm good for as many orgasms as you can handle. Actually, I'm *great* at that."

"True. Anything else?"

"I'm possessive. No one else touches you. Nonnegotiable."

"That works for me," I say, my overheated body making me impatient. "Anything else?"

"I'm good at protecting you. No one better fuck with you now that we're together. I promise you that. I'm good at providing for you. I'll give you my credit card. You can have whatever you want—"

"I don't want or need your money." My God, why won't he *listen*? "I just told you that."

"But you're getting it! That's the point!" He seems to realize he's shouting and takes a deep breath. "That's one of the few things I can do. I can give you the world. Let me do it. And you'd better believe that all that—everything I just said—adds up to me being your man or your boyfriend or your *boo*. Whatever label you want to put on it. But I'd better not hear you acting like I'm no big deal to you with your father. Because that's going to piss me off."

"Great," I say, marveling at his ability to bark out the most romantic things and make them sound like an NFL coach roaring strategies to his players on the field during overtime at the Super Bowl. "Anything else you want me to know? While you're barking out directives?"

"Yeah. Don't expect me to vomit up all my pain and all my feelings and all my hopes and dreams about the future. I'm not that guy. You'd be wasting your time. There's nothing else to me other than what I just told you. The sooner you get that through your stubborn skull, the happier we'll both be."

"You're so full of shit," I say before I can stop myself. Insensitive? Maybe. He clearly believes what he's saying. That doesn't mean *I* have to.

He cocks his head then goes completely still. *"What?"*

"Bullshit." A funny thing happens when I meet all that

anger head-on and stare straight into those flashing eyes. I catch an unexpected glimpse of the vulnerability underneath. The thing he's trying so desperately to hide. "I don't believe you."

"You don't believe me? I just told you exactly what kind of guy I am, and *you don't believe me*?" His tone suggests he's caught me washing my hair with bleach. "Based on what?"

It's a valid question. If a friend of mine were in this exact situation and came to me for advice, I'd drive her to the nearest priest so she could exorcise that man and that demon, Temptation, from her life as soon as possible. But all the normal dating rules don't feel like they apply to me and Griffin, for reasons that remain elusive now. I can't shake the feeling that I'm not trying to change him into someone else. I'm just trying to break through to the man he really is. Maybe that's a distinction without a difference. Maybe I'm doomed to failure either way.

But it doesn't feel like it. It really doesn't feel like it.

"I don't know," I say. "A gut feeling. Women's intuition. Maybe some undiagnosed head injury. I have no idea. But I think there's more here. And I'm not giving up on you."

His expression goes through a constellation of emotions. It might be a symptom of my creeping insanity, but I'd swear I detect as much hope and relief as anger and frustration. Hell, I don't know. Maybe they all cancel each other out, leaving me exactly where I started from with this maddening man.

But I don't think so.

"That's on you, then." His face is hard now, his features set in marble. "Because I warned you. And we've done enough talking."

Finally. Something we can easily agree on. Especially when he gives my cute little sundress the same treatment he gave his shirt, ripping the two halves apart and exposing my strapless bra in all its lacy glory. Not to mention my bare bottom half.

I laugh. I can't help it. I know it's twisted to take such delight in his shaking hands, dark intent and raw urgency, but I do. I revel in the way he impatiently undoes my bra's front clasp and tosses it aside so he can savor my breasts with a rumble of masculine appreciation. I rejoice at the feeling of his rough caress across my nipples.

There's no way I can hide any of it. I don't even want to.

So I don't try to hold back the way his name pours out of my mouth with exquisite anguish. I give him everything, leaning back on my hands to arch my back and offer up any part of me that he cares to nuzzle, lick, kiss, rub or bite. Thorough as ever, he hits it all, starting with a bang as he scrapes his teeth across the sensitive tendons where neck meets shoulder and working his way down. He cups my breasts, squeezing, massaging and generally manhandling them. Normally, a bit of finesse goes much farther for me, but not this time. The direct connection between his frenzy and the spiraling pleasure pooling between my legs makes me happy with anything and everything he does. Especially when he grips my hips, rubs his face over my belly and drops to his knees in front of me, settling my thighs on his shoulders.

I don't know what makes him pause at that electric moment—as though I'd squawk with modesty and tell him I'm not that type of girl—but he stares up the length of my body, the flash of his blue eyes startling against my pale skin and pointy pink nipples.

"Go ahead," I say with a laugh that has more than a tinge of wild euphoria to it. "You won't be happy until you take it all, anyway. And I won't be happy until I give it to you."

"Damn straight," he says, and there's no missing his glimmer of grim satisfaction before he lowers his head.

So there I am, squirming and splayed on the counter with my dress ripped half off, knocking over toiletries and moaning my fool head off while he eats me out. He effortlessly finds that single most delicious spot, zeroing in on my clit as though it contains a homing beacon just for him. Which would explain why others have tried and failed to find this spot and resisted my increasingly frustrated efforts to guide them there. He savors my pussy with lush and lapping strokes, finding a rhythm that leads to one inevitable result:

My high-pitched cry of astonished relief as my orgasm escapes from my body on an endless surge of pleasure, like the eruption of some sensual volcano.

Enough heat lingers in my cheeks to mark my sudden embarrassment as he rises to his feet and nuzzles his way back up my torso. I don't know what I'm going to say after *that*. But *he* does all the talking, whispering to me between fevered kisses that now taste like fresh oysters.

"I can't get enough of you," he says. "I want you more every time I hear that sound."

"I don't know what it is about you." I can't hold back a shaky laugh. "You've got me making sounds I've never made before."

"*I* know what it is," he says, gripping my waist and

helping me stand on my wobbly legs before turning me around.

Now we both face the mirror, my back to his front with the two halves of my dress forming curtains for my otherwise naked body, and the sight of all this raw abandon is erotic, of course, but also startling and surprisingly stirring. We both have high color, tousled hair and swollen lips. No surprises there. But there's something about the way his big body encases my smaller one that really gets to me. Something about the tender yet possessive way his roving hands stroke over my engorged breasts, letting my nipples poke through his splayed fingers. Something about the sweep of those same fingers across the ruddy pink skin between my pale thighs.

When he holds me this tightly and loves me this thoroughly, it doesn't seem so crazy to believe him when he says he'll give me anything I want or need. That he'll protect me.

When he touches me like this and I see that blaze of intensity in his blue eyes, I know I'm in this for the long haul. Whatever that means, whatever form that takes. If he wants me, I'm here.

"You do?" I ask. "Don't keep me in suspense."

"We're making up for lost time," he says, keeping an eye on me in the mirror as he nips my neck, making me squirm. "We should've been like this from the beginning."

"That would've gotten my vote. But you never noticed me."

"Bullshit. I noticed you. I wanted you. Exactly like this."

Music to my ears. I've always wondered. Especially

given the way he's noticed every other woman who's crossed his path during that time.

"Like this?" I say, grinding my ass against the hard length of his dick and enjoying the way he tenses in response. Then I turn, push him back a step, drop to my knees and look past his heaving chest to his downturned face as he watches me with avid interest. "Or like *this*?"

"Whatever you want to give me," he says, his voice hoarse. He takes my head in his hands, strokes my hair and massages my scalp. "I'm there."

"Glad to hear it," I say before taking him in my hands and putting my mouth on him.

I grip and squeeze. I cup his balls. I stroke. I lick. I suck, taking him deep. I work him hard, my mouth straining to manage his plump head and thick length. He groans above me. Whispers urgent words of encouragement that I can't quite hear before finally pulling my hair to get me to stop. But I take my time releasing him, making sure to maintain eye contact as I slowly let him slide free.

"Get up here," he says, taking my hands and pulling me up.

His touch is rough as he turns me to face the mirror again. Urgent. He bends me over the counter, making sure my hands are planted just the way he wants them. Brushes my leg with his knee in a silent command to widen my stance. I'm only too happy to comply, especially when he strokes my slick cleft with his fingers and then his dick. As if there's some outside chance that I'm not wet and creamy enough to accommodate him by now. I hold my breath, waiting for him to grip my hips, adjust the angle and get it right…

"*Hurry,*" I say, agonized, and he enters me with a

sharp thrust that makes me cry out with exquisite pleasure.

My eyes roll closed. His breath hisses. Honest to God, I feel as though I'm sliding into some altered state, some sexual Twilight Zone where every experience is thrillingly abnormal, but I force my heavy lids open again, determined to experience this moment with all of my senses. Especially sight.

The scene is raw and unfiltered as he begins to move inside me with hard and rhythmic pumps of his hips. Animalistic. Both of our faces are red and strained. Muscles flex in his arms and across his torso. My hair swings in my face. My breasts dangle. He grunts. I moan as the pleasure cements itself between my thighs. We watch each other the entire time, our eyes locked in the mirror.

We are wild and unrestrained together. We are *sexy*.

And the sight of his heavy-lidded gaze and the way his features twist with gathering ecstasy as he presses his face to my neck? Absolutely unforgettable.

"I'm going to fuck you like this. All summer." His eyes flick open again, nailing me with a look of dark intent. "We have to burn this out before you leave."

I can only put a little more effort into my counterthrusting and laugh at his foolishness. As if I'm going to go gently when the fall comes. As if either one of us could ever overcome *this*.

"You can try all you want." I have no idea where my new breathless sex-kitten routine comes from. I only know that it feels as though I'm speaking from the bottom of my soul. And if it sounds a little like a curse on him, even to my own ears, well, so be it. "But you're not getting me out of your system. There's no way."

He doesn't like this. I can tell by the way his nostrils flare. And then, as predictable as the tides, Griffin does what he always does: offers new sexual diversion.

He smacks my hip with one hand, palms my breasts with the other, closes his eyes again and gives himself over to the moment, sounding anguished as he shouts my name.

But I spoke the truth just now. And we both know it.

He stiffens, his big body spasming against me as he holds me tighter. *Tighter.* I wish we could freeze time right here in this moment, where we know what matters and what doesn't. I wonder how many more times we'll butt heads and who will emerge the victor.

I wonder if a man like this could ever fall in love with me.

The tension eventually eases from his body. I see his eyes flick open in the mirror. Electric blue. Sapphires and diamonds.

"I keep wondering," he says quietly, running his lips across the top of my back. He's still trying to catch his breath.

"Wondering what?" I ask.

"When you're finally going to get tired of my bull-shit." There's a long pause while his gaze wavers. I get the feeling he doesn't want to reveal the full extent of his dark thoughts. "Walk out on me."

I choose my words carefully. This feels crucial. I can't get it wrong.

"That depends. Are you trying to drive me away?"

Shaky laugh from Griffin. "I'd like to think I'm smarter than that. I know it's questionable sometimes, but…"

"Hmmm. I'm inclined to give you a chance. Would that be a waste of my time?"

We stare at each other for several long beats. He swallows hard, making his Adam's apple bob and revealing a depth of vulnerability that makes my heart ache. Takes a deep breath.

"No."

"Good," I say, relieved. So is he, judging by the way his eyes crinkle at the corners. "I think I'm going to grab my credit card and go order that pizza. I'm starving. I seem to have worked up an appetite."

Griffin scowls. "This is a test, isn't it?"

"Absolutely," I say. "Proceed carefully."

He heaves an aggrieved sigh and gives my shoulder a final kiss.

"Whatever you want. Just make sure my half is pineapple-free."

16

GRIFFIN—TWO MONTHS LATER

I'M INTO BELLAMY. Big time. I don't deny it.

But my dire prognosis doesn't sink in until late one night toward the end of the summer, when I gratefully tiptoe into my apartment after a week of meetings in Singapore. My gratitude at being back home with her creates a pang in the center of my chest that's almost as painful as the ache of loneliness I felt without her these last several days. There's something about knowing she's in my apartment, waiting for me. Something about the sensation of coming home *to her*. It does funny things to my head. Makes me think crazy thoughts.

For example?

What if I whisked her away to, say, Barbados for the weekend? Raised the issue of trying to make things work long distance?

Insane, right? Long-distance relationships rarely work, and when they do, it's gotta be with a guy way more emotionally evolved than me. Bellamy deserves a clean break and a fresh start out west with a good guy. Someone who deserves her. Someone who knows how to open up and let his partner into his life in a meaningful way.

Someone who's the opposite of *me*, in other words.

The idea makes me feel dead and rotted on the inside, but I'm not the important one here.

She is.

But…

Is this what it's like for other guys when they come back home, even when it's to a largely furniture-free apartment like mine? Do normal guys in healthy relationships get this kind of break from the yawning emptiness inside? More to the point, do they even feel the kind of emptiness I felt until Bellamy exploded into my personal life?

Hell, I don't know. I'd need to bring in someone way smarter than I am to answer questions like that.

I don't believe in *falling in love*, whatever that means. I especially don't believe in falling in love with someone when you know going in that their time in your life will be shorter than a baseball season. But times like this, when I feel as though I can't manage another breath without seeing her again, remind me that I need to remind myself that love is for fairytales and for people who don't mind looking foolish.

In other words, not me.

But tell that to my thumping and lonely heart.

I enter my apartment and stop cold. Why? Because the scene is far too good to be true. Like a dream. Actually, strike that. It's like somebody else's dream.

When I left on Sunday, my furniture consisted of a leather sofa, a two-person kitchen table and a king-sized bed in the master. A giant TV. That's all I needed. Why bother with more? I'm always at the office or traveling anyway.

Now?

The place looks as though it's been commandeered by some high-octane home-makeover show and turned it into a soothing sanctuary in pale gray and black.

I take it all in as I set my bags down, too stunned to hike my bottom jaw off the floor.

I've got sectionals. Coffee tables with coffee table books on them. Chairs. End tables. Lamps. Matching rugs, blankets, pillows and all the little tchotchkes that go with making a place into a home. There are gorgeous abstract paintings on the wall and—I squint, overcome with disbelief—silver-framed pictures of me and my brothers sitting on a console. Wonder of wonders, I've also got a real dining room table for adults. With matching chairs, a funky modern chandelier, a sculptured centerpiece and everything.

I can't fucking believe it. One touch of Bellamy's magical hands and the place, which has been exactly as welcoming as an empty warehouse with nice windows and a great view, has become a haven that I'll probably never want to leave again.

And where is the architect of all this change?

Curled on her side under a blanket over on the sectional, dead asleep with the drowsy dog draped over her hip. She's got a hand under her chin, intensifying the innocent effect. Hard to believe a woman capable of flipping every part of my life upside down and inside out can look that angelic. But anyone who tolerates my bullshit with such grace and good humor is, by definition, an angel.

I stare down at her, drowning in questions.

What goes on in that head of hers? Does she dream about me? Does she wonder what we're going to do when the clock runs out on our time together? Or is she counting down the days until she's done with me once and for all? Does she think I'm going to want to come home to this wonderful haven she's created for me once she moves across the country and won't be here to greet me when I walk in the door?

And if she *does* think that — *is she insane?*

Too many questions. No answers.

Jeremy yawns, stretches, hops down and trots over to give me a welcoming sniff.

"Hey, buddy," I said quietly, scooping him into a football hold so I can ruffle his ears. "How're you doing?"

The dog gives me one of his bright-eyed smiles, wiggles happily and licks my hand. Instant stress relievers that will also be unavailable after the Big Move.

I kiss his furry forehead, set him down and head for my new drink cart. Which Bellamy has, naturally, fully stocked with nice new crystal tumblers and my favorite gin and tonic water.

I pour liberally and sip long and appreciatively. I'm considering the relative wisdom of topping the glass off again when I hear her stir.

"Hey," she says in the throaty *just woke up* voice that's a close second to the sound of her coming for me in terms of sexiest sounds in the world. "Why didn't you wake me up?"

I turn to watch her sit up and stretch, my heartbeat a dull thump in my throat. "I thought I'd let you sleep for a minute."

"Yeah?"

"I'm thoughtful like that. Get over here."

She gets up and heads over, revealing a tiny pink satin robe that barely reaches the tops of her sweet thighs. The heavy curves of her breasts and prominent points of her nipples are on display. Her swaying hips and shapely legs are on display. She hits me with the steady beam from those luminous eyes. A sultry smile.

And I am lost.

I set my drink down, freeing both arms to pull her in close. The overwhelming relief at finally being able to touch her again sends a shudder through my body. She feels so warm and solid. Her skin is still velvety soft and smells like roses. That hasn't changed. Thank God it hasn't changed.

I breathe her in, squeezing her hard enough now to make up for all the nights when I wanted to but couldn't.

And she squeezes back.

"Did you miss me?" she asks.

I open up enough daylight between us to reach into my pocket, withdraw a jade bangle and slide it onto her wrist as she gasps with surprise.

"Not at all," I say, my words wedging themselves in my throat. My mouth is full of things I can't tell her. Like how the jewelry store in the lobby of my swanky hotel called my name all week and finally insisted that I spend the better part of a late afternoon trying to decide what to bring back for her. Or the way I examined every bracelet, bangle and bobble the place had, becoming an expert on jade in the process. I can never tell her that I felt an unnatural fascination with the side of the store that displayed engagement rings and had a difficult time not wandering over to see what was what.

Even if I wanted to tell her these things, which I don't, the words feel as though they're locked in maximum security deep inside my own personal Rikers Island. I don't know why I have so many walls and barriers surrounding me on every side. And I have zero idea how to access the treasure trove of secrets I've got buried in all my dark corners. Which is probably a good thing when you consider what I really want to tell her.

Let's work something out. I can't picture my life without you.

And above all?

Don't leave.

"This is *gorgeous*," she says, stretching out her arm to admire the bangle. "Thank you."

Another thing to add to my Cannot Say list?

I live for your smile, Bellamy.

Live. For. It.

"Glad you like it." I turn away and reach for my drink again as a distraction, then sip without tasting.

"How was your flight?" she asks.

"Long."

"Poor baby. Are you hungry? I saved some—"

As if I could choke down some food right now. "I'm fine."

The silence that follows is awkward enough for me to risk a glance at her. I catch her just as she hitches her smile back into place.

That's me, folks. I never met a conversation I couldn't sour or a mood I couldn't ruin.

"Everything okay?" she asks carefully.

"Yep." I try to sound more upbeat, but upbeat and I go together like a squid and a mountain bike. "Just need a shower and some sleep."

I start for the bathroom—

"Griffin," she says behind me, the wounded note in

her voice clearly audible. "How do you like your apartment?"

I freeze. I know what she needs, but I'm incapable—or unwilling—to open myself up enough to give it to her. It's like I've built a brick factory somewhere inside my brain, cranked it up to full capacity and required all the workers to put in double overtime to make sure the wall keeps growing as tall as possible. Otherwise? I'm afraid of what might come out of my mouth. Worst-case scenario? I open up enough to tell her that in my entire life no one has given me such a loving and meaningful gift as decorating my apartment and out springs something like *I still don't believe in love but I think I'm falling in love with you* or *I seriously think I'll die if you disappear from my life the way my mother disappeared from my life.*

And what would happen then?

Confusion. Chaos. Some sort of personal Armageddon, the outlines of which I can't quite comprehend now. I only know that it would be *bad*, and I don't want to risk it.

"It's good." I make a show of looking around as though I've just noticed everything for the first time. This sorry performance is the best I can do. "Thanks."

With that, I take off for the bathroom, congratulating myself on a respectable performance while pretending I don't see her crestfallen expression.

I linger in the shower's driving spray for as long as I possibly can, well past the point where my scalded skin resembles a boiled lobster. My thoughts don't clear. By the time I towel off and head to the bedroom—I don't bother with pajama bottoms when I'm in bed with Bellamy; never have, never will—I'm both physically and emotionally exhausted but too wired to sleep. I've never been one for pills, not that one would work on me tonight anyway. The way I'm feeling, nothing short of a shot from an elephant tranquilizer gun would do the trick. Still, I've got to close my eyes. Just for a little bit.

Bellamy's already in bed (she's worked her decorating magic in here, too), stretched out on her side and facing away from me. Just enough moonlight filters through the drapes to hit the top of her head where it rests on the pillow and create a gleaming beacon for me to follow. I climb in behind her and eagerly spoon her up into our nightly position, with her round ass settled in my lap, my top arm draped around her waist and my nose buried in her hair as I root for the warmth of her scent. Given my performance in the living room a few minutes ago, I half expect her to kick me out of bed and doom me to a miserable night out on the sofa with one of her new decorator pillows and blankets.

But she doesn't.

To my eternal gratitude, she snuggles closer and puts her soft hand on top of my arm. I say a million silent prayers of gratitude and kiss her shoulder. It takes everything I've got not to let my hand stray higher or lower, which she can no doubt tell from the size of my erection. I'm dying to fuck her again, but I don't want to press my luck.

"I missed you," she says quietly. "I have no idea why."

This information should make me feel happy. Instead, it only makes me feel bleak. A spectacular woman like Bellamy deserves so much more than a jackass like me.

"You shouldn't," I tell her. "I'm not worth it."

"That's for me to decide."

My exhaustion, the lateness of the hour and the fact

that we're not looking at each other create the perfect
storm to allow me to confide for second. Just enough to
share one of my biggest fears.

"You *will* decide I'm not worth it. It's only a matter of
time."

There's a long pause.

"You've got to give me something to work with, Griffin," she says, and I'd swear tears have a sound, because
I hear them in her voice. "I can't hold this relationship up
all by myself."

Does she think I don't know that? Doesn't she
understand that if I could access the part of me that's
locked behind a wall, broken and probably ruined, I
would?

"Tell me how and I *will*," I say.

"You need to figure that out for yourself. And I need
to figure out if there's any way for me to stick around
without getting my heart broken."

A shiver of alarm runs through me. I don't like the
sound of that at all.

"Bellamy—"

"Go to sleep," she tells me, pulling away and making
me regret my choice of a king-sized bed. "I'm tired."

I want to pull her back, but I don't dare. Not if I
want to keep both of my arms. I flop over onto my back
and give my pillow a frustrated whack, trying to get
comfortable by myself. Which I used to be able to do, in
the Before Bellamy period of my life.

I drift off after a good amount of blearily staring at
the far wall, but it's a restless, exhaustion-fueled sleep.
The kind that's more like watching TV all night than
getting any rest. So it's no surprise when I slide into my
childhood nightmare.

The setting? A horror movie version of the west wing of our house in the Hamptons. More like a cavern that a home, ominously dark, with only enough light to generate shadows and obstacles out of the looming furniture. I fumble along with my arms outstretched, looking for my mother. Even in the dream, I'm ashamed of my terror. A little kid searching in the dark for his mommy. You're kidding, right? That's the best you can do? You can't even generate a bogeyman?

But the dream is plenty scary enough without the bogeyman, thanks. It's not just the lack of my mother that does it to me. It's the lack of *anyone*.

I hit a wall. Ricochet off in another direction. Stumble into something, generating a stabbing pain that starts in my knee and shoots out the top of my head. I stifle my cry of pain because it seems important to keep quiet and not wake anything that might be lurking in the darkness. I limp around, wondering why I can't find any familiar landmarks, and hit another wall.

Out in the darkness, something rumbles. An animal. A demon. A monster. Whatever it is, I never want to find out.

That's why all hell breaks loose in my terrified little kid mind.

"Where is everybody?" I shout, breaking into as much of a run as I dare in the gloom. "You can't just leave me like this!"

Something moves beside me, heightening my panic.

A distant voice speaks. "Griffin?"

"Why would you leave me like this? Why would you — Wait. *Is someone there? Hello?*"

"Griffin? Wake up."

Something grips my arm. I yelp with surprise and jolt myself awake, my entire body spasming.

"Griffin. It's okay."

The nightmare quickly dissipates, leaving me with an erratic heartbeat and a scream choked off in my throat. So that makes things fun. As does the fact that I'm drenched in a cold sweat and still shaky. It'll be hard to act like a competent professional now that I've been reduced to my worst childhood fears in front of Bellamy. Who, by the way, is currently watching me with the kind of open concern that sets my teeth on edge. Given the choice between being a beast and a basket case, I'll choose the asshole option every day and twice on Sundays.

She leans closer and massages my back, the silky curtain of her hair tickling my arm.

"What happened?"

"That should be obvious," I say as I rub my hands over my face, pulling away because I don't want *pity*. Not from Bellamy. "I had a nightmare."

"I'd pieced that much together," she says acidly. "Do you want to talk about it?"

I drop my hands and gape at her. "Do I *want to talk about it*? Have we met?"

She tenses. If I squint right, I can almost see the reins of her control slipping through her fingers.

"How about a simple *no*?" she says.

"How about you just stop asking. Any question that centers around me talking about something is going to have *no* as the answer. *No*. We don't need to deconstruct my nightmare about being trapped in the west wing. Let it go."

I get up, reach for the robe I keep at the end of the

bed, slide it on and wonder how bad I'd have to act to get an explosion out of her. And then I wonder why I need this explosion so badly.

"There's a saying. *Monsters live in the dark.*"

"Come on, Bellamy."

"Maybe it's past time for you to start shining some light on your monsters," she says.

I don't know why I feel so dangerously unhinged. Or why she's so determined to highlight all my weaknesses, as though she doesn't see them on full display already. Whatever it is, I can't fight the urge to rub her face in it. Make her open her eyes and *see*.

"Maybe *I'm* the monster, Bellamy. Maybe that's why you call me *the Beast*. Ever think of that?"

"Yeah, I've thought about it," she says, making me wince with both her words and the directness of her gaze. "But I don't think you are. I think it's a defense mechanism."

That hits way too close to home.

"Jesus Christ. Now you're a shrink?"

"Either that or a fool," she says grimly.

I snort. "Your words. Not mine."

"Do you *want* me to leave?" The quiet reproach in her tone slices through my bullshit like a hot samurai sword through a stick of butter, leaving me wounded and ashamed. Her silent condemnation is a million times more effective than the authoritative voice I use at the office. A million times worse than any explosion could ever be. "If that's what you're going for here, why not just say so?"

That's when it hits me in a moment of clarity so stunning that it almost knocks me on my ass.

I *do* want her to leave. I want her to leave now so I

won't have to keep living with the terror of knowing she *will* inevitably leave. The dread is killing me. I can't take it for another minute of another day. And I can't keep falling deeper under her spell when I know she's going to rip my heart out with her absence.

"Oh my God," she says, eyes widening. I've never been a good actor, and any skills I've developed over the years are worthless at a high-stakes moment like this. "You *do* want me to leave."

I open my mouth to tell her…*something*. But, surprise of surprises, I've got no words. Just that fucking brick wall.

Her phone pings and lights up on her nightstand, startling us both. She glances around, frowning, while I check my watch. Two fourteen.

My dread intensifies. This can't be good.

"That's my father," she says, then lunges for it and answers midway through the second ring. "Daddy? What's wrong?"

She listens, her frown deepening. I hurry over to her side of the bed, take her free hand and give it a supportive squeeze. She shoots me a weak smile.

"But you didn't hit your head?" More listening. "So when is the surgery? Okay. Okay. I'll be there soon as I can. Of course I'm coming. *Daddy*. I'm not arguing with you. Okay. I'll keep you posted. Okay. Okay. Love you. Bye."

She hangs up, tosses the phone on the bed and rubs her upper arms.

"He got up on the stepladder to get a snack from the cabinet," she says, sounding a little shaky. "*Cheetos*. He missed a step on the way down and landed hard. Sounds like he splintered his ankle like a dry twig. He needs surgery."

"Ouch. Sounds painful."

"No kidding."

"Cheetos are a worthy snack, though."

She manages a weak smile. "Not sure he'll agree once he has a bunch of pins stuck in his leg and has to stay off his feet for several weeks."

My brain cranks into problem-solving mode. If he needs anything, I plan to make sure he has it.

"Several weeks? What about his landscaping work?"

"I don't know," she says helplessly. "I haven't gotten that far yet."

"Has he got health insurance?"

"Yeah. Thank God. I have to go."

"I know. You can take the jet."

"Oh, I couldn't—"

"Take the jet."

"Thanks," she says after a pause, rubbing her chest. "I want to be there when he comes out of surgery."

"Of course you do."

"I don't know how long I'll be gone," she says, grabbing her clothes from the chair and starting to change. "I'm not sure how long they'll want to keep him and what will be involved with making his little house accessible. It's just one story, but he's got steps. I guess he'll need a ramp for the time being if he's in a wheelchair. He doesn't have anyone nearby since his brother died last year. And I don't see him letting the neighbors help. He's too proud and stubborn for that."

"Understood."

"But I don't want to be gone too long, because we

still need to interview and train my replacement, and we only have three weeks left. Oh, but I have my orientation for law school, too. I forgot about that." She stares off in the distance for several beats, brow furrowed, then snaps back into my trusted Girl Friday. "Don't worry. I'll get it figured out. I'd never leave you in the lurch."

I say nothing. My brain is too full of images of Bellamy flying back and forth while she tries to manage my life and her father's while also closing up her apartment here, getting settled out west and getting her mind right for the beginning of school.

I may be a demanding SOB of a boss, but even I'm not that bad.

That's when the second moment of clarity of the night hits me with the force of a lightning strike to my soul. It's time for me to do the right thing. Not the right thing for *me*, which would probably involve something wildly possessive and permanent, like handcuffing us together and swallowing the key so that Bellamy can stay on my right side forever, but the right thing for *her*. Time for me to recognize that the end of the summer brings the end of my own personal paradise with it. We had our time together, but we knew going in that this thing had a deadline. Like all deadlines, it came a whole lot quicker than I'd have liked, but it's here now. Time for me to free Bellamy up to live her best life out west.

I just hope I have the balls to do it.

As for me? I'll be okay. Eventually. There's no need to act like I'll be cursed with loneliness for the rest of my life. I managed to live for thirty-two years without her and I did fine. Hopefully, the skill is like riding a bike.

"You okay?" she asks me. "We need to get this

figured out. I just want to do the right thing by you at the office."

"And I plan to do the right thing by *you*," I say, suddenly unable to meet her gaze. "No matter what."

17

BELLAMY

"I JUST NEED A FEW MINUTES," I tell Griffin half an hour or so later, when he takes me back to my apartment to pack my carry-on bag. "I always keep my travel toiletries stocked, so it won't take me long. I don't want to keep the pilot waiting."

"The pilot flies when you're ready." He shuts the door behind us and takes a good look at the boxes I now have stacked around the perimeter of my living room, which are a new development since he was here last. "What's all this?"

"Oh, I forgot to mention," I say, tossing my bag on the sofa. "I made a lot of progress this week while you were gone."

"I see that." He maintains his alarming new practice of not looking me in the eye as he settles on the sofa and rests his elbows on his knees. He stares down at his hands and rubs them together, saying nothing.

"I don't like to procrastinate," I continue. "Especially when I have a big job. Like moving."

"I know."

Still no eye contact.

I'm so worried about my father right now that I should have zero room left for other emotions. Wrong. Griffin keeps acting funny, which means I'm also dealing with fear tightening my throat and prickling across the nape of my neck. I don't know what's on his mind—nothing new there—but I know it's nothing good.

"Thanks again for keeping Jeremy for me while I'm gone," I say, shoving my hands into the pockets of my jeans and shifting nervously. I'm having a tough time standing still. I know my nerves are making me babble, but there's nothing I can do about it. "I really appreciate that. Makes my life much easier."

"Happy to have him."

"Grab something to drink if you want it. I'll be right back."

"Yep."

I linger in the doorway, but Griffin seems as determined to ignore me as I am to get him to say something. *Anything.* But I'd have a better chance of success if I tried to ride my bike to the moon. Besides, we don't have all night and it would take a hell of a lot longer than that for me to figure out what goes through Griffin's mind. That being the case, I head to the bedroom, retrieve my carry-on from the closet and start throwing things inside.

Jeans. Tops. Toiletries. Shoes. Undies.

What am I forgetting, though? I feel like I'm forgetting something—

Ella. That's it. I need to let her know what's going on. Since it's the middle of the night, the civilized thing to do would be to text her. But my simmering fear prevents me from feeling very civilized right now. I need my best

friend's advice, bottom line. So I hurry into the bathroom, shut the door and pull out my phone.

"Hello?" she says groggily. The picture resolves to
show her sitting up in bed and pushing her messy hair
away from her face. "Bellamy? What's wrong?"

"Sorry to wake you up. Where's Ryker?"

"He's in London for meetings. What's going on? Did
something happen?"

"Yeah. My dad stumbled off his stepladder and broke
his ankle in a million places. He needs surgery. I'm
heading out there now."

"Oh, no," she says, leaning over to click on her lamp.
The worry in her expression perfectly matches the way I
feel inside. "Will he be okay?"

"I think so. But he's going to have a long rehab. And
I don't know what this means for his landscaping business. Or for him being in his little house by himself."

"Oh, true. What a mess. And right before your move
and starting school."

"Exactly."

"Do you need me to watch Jeremy for you?"

"No. Griffin's got him."

"Hey, yeah," she says around a jaw-splitting yawn.
"What's going on with you and Griffin?"

"No idea," I say glumly. "We have three weeks left
together, and now my father's situation is cutting into
that time. Meanwhile, Griffin hasn't said one word about
next steps or trying the long-distance thing or anything
like that. And he's acting strange tonight. He barely
commented on the apartment redo. I'm afraid he's about
to dump me."

"Well…" She adopts the gentle tone of someone
about to deliver dire news. *You're going to have to replace*

your entire septic system, ma'am. "This was always supposed to be a summer fling, right?"

Like I want to think about *that* at this dark moment.

"Thanks for the reminder."

"Wait a minute." She squints and takes a closer look at me, looking scandalized. "You didn't fall in love with him, did you? Bellamy! He's not as big a jerk as I thought he was, but he's not the kind of guy you get serious about. If nothing else, he's a known player. What're you *doing*?"

The L-word is a blow. Sure, it's been tiptoeing around the periphery of my thoughts for weeks and creeping right up to the tip of my tongue, waiting for the right moment to slip out. Like when we laugh together. Or when we fall asleep tangled up in each other's arms and legs. Or when he looks at me with that aching vulnerability in those blue eyes. Or when he expects me not to notice the way he stares at me when we're together. I doubt I could so much as shed an eyelash without him noticing.

I think I love you, Griffin.

I think I'm crazy in love with you.

It's right there, waiting, but I haven't said it.

And it's a good thing. Why? Because he's never said anything about love, ever. Other than his stated position, which is that love is not a thing.

The grave truth is that I've fallen for a man who doesn't share his feelings. Or let me in. Or talk about the future. Or believe in love.

He's a real winner, boy. An emotional apex predator. The great white shark of the romance world.

And I'm just foolish enough to ignore all the flashing warning signs.

Hang on. That's not entirely true. It's not that I don't see or care about the warning signs. It's just that his good qualities seem so much more important.

I know that plenty of people out there would swear on a stack of Bibles that he's never displayed *any* good qualities. They may have a point. But I've glimpsed humor in him. Intelligence. Kindness. Tenderness. And sexiness? Don't get me started.

But the question on the table is: have I fallen in love with the entire Griffin Black package?

Yeah. I really think I have. And there's no *think* about it.

I'm crazy in love with you, Griffin. Let's try the long-distance thing. I'm willing to be flexible with my plans so I can keep you in my life. I want you. I need you. I love you.

Straight up, no chaser.

Not that I'm ready to admit it aloud.

So I try to laugh it off.

"Love? What're you talking about? I'm fine. Do I care about him more than I expected to? Yeah. But no one said anything about *love*."

"You don't have to. It's written all over your face."

"That's ridiculous," I say, my morale plummeting to subterranean levels. Things are worse than I'd feared if she can wake from a dead sleep, take one look at me and diagnose me with a raging case of the L-word. "And I've got to go catch my flight."

"What are you going to do about Griffin?"

I shrug. "Like I know."

"Whatever you do, *please* don't throw yourself at him," she says. "Don't get clingy. Men hate that. It drives them away every time. Be smart."

Smart and I parted ways the second I first made a

move on Griffin, alas. Now I seem to be flying on blind instinct. Not a foolproof plan, I admit.

"The thing is…I think there's something here. Or could be if I can just get past his brick walls."

She gapes at me as though I've sprouted a pig's snout. "Says every lovestruck woman ever, Bellamy."

"I know. But my gut keeps telling me I've got to stick with him. I can't give up. Not yet."

She smacks her forehead, scrunches up her face, slowly opens her eyes again and takes a deep breath.

My heart sinks even further.

"I want to be supportive. I really do," she says. "I just don't understand what makes you feel so sure."

I struggle for a minute, words failing me.

"It's the way I catch him looking at me sometimes. Like I'm a miracle. Like he's won the lottery. It's the way he lights up when I walk into the room. It's the way he's changed since we got together. It's like he glows from the inside. It's the vibe I get from him sometimes. It's needy. Hopeful. Vulnerable. I don't know if I'm making any sense."

"You're making sense, Bells, but that's what every woman says about the bad boy who's never going to change for her. You know that."

"I know," I say glumly. "I've probably got some form of Stockholm syndrome."

We share a weak laugh.

"Look," she says. "I don't want to squash all your hopes and dreams. Maybe he *is* your prince. If you really think he is, then go for it."

My ears perk up. "What do you mean?" I say, my heart beginning to thump with excitement.

"I mean, tell him how you feel. Lay all your cards on the table. Go big or go home —"

"You *just* said —"

"I know I did, but I also know how you are. You'll never be satisfied unless you give it your best shot. And if it doesn't work out, at least you'll know you tried. So you can move on with the rest of your life with no regrets."

"Funny you should say that. I just got an email from my contact at the admissions office at NYU."

"What? The one you had such a great interview with? Who was so disappointed that you went with Berkeley?"

"Yes. She said she was just checking in and wants me to call her if I ever need anything or if I decide I'm not happy at Berkeley. She didn't come right out and say it, but I had the feeling that she'd help me transfer after the first semester if I decided I wasn't happy at Berkeley."

Ella looks impressed. "That's amazing. So there's your opening with Griffin."

"That's what I was kinda thinking, yeah," I say, afraid to get my hopes up too high. "Is this an insane idea? What do you think?"

"I think you'd be insane not to go with your gut and do what you need to do to be happy."

"Thanks," I say, my relieved smile threatening to swallow my entire face. Ella's support and encouragement mean the world to me. Always have. If she thinks this is possible, then it really is. As long as Griffin's willing to meet me halfway and give this a chance, that's all I need. "Wish me luck."

"Good luck. Keep me posted."

"I will. Love you. Bye."

"Bye."

I finish packing and take my carry-on out to the living room, where I discover Griffin exactly as he was, still staring down at his hands. Actually, there's something new this time: a muscle flexing in his tight jaw. The sight of all this tension does nothing to soothe my nerves and kicks off another round of babbling.

"Ready whenever you are," I say. "Thanks again for letting me take the jet. And for holding down the forts with Jeremy and at the office until I get back. I run a tight ship, so I'd better not come back to chaos and turmoil. I'm warning you now."

He clears his throat as he stands and takes the handle of my carry-on. "Noted. Let's go."

No eye contact. None whatsoever.

The idea of driving to the airport and then leaving for several days with this cloud of uncertainty over my head feels like a death sentence. I can't take it for another second.

"Griffin. What the hell is going on? And don't tell me *nothing*."

He hesitates, each millisecond shaving a year off my life.

"It's nothing to get into right now," he says finally. "We'll talk about it after your dad gets out of surgery. You've got enough on your plate right now."

Like he's doing me some huge favor by prolonging this suffering.

"If you care anything about my plate, then start talking," I say. "Because the way you're acting is spiking my blood pressure."

He lets go of my carry-on and heaves one of those long-suffering sighs that men always produce when women force them into difficult conversations. Then he runs his hands over the top of his head, ruffling his hair, and looks me in the eyes, and it's written all over his face in some sort of emotional permanent marker. In giant black letters.

My heart craters long before he opens his mouth and gets his words going.

"Don't, ah… Don't worry about coming back here," he says quietly. "Your father needs you now. Stay with him. I'll arrange to have everything in your apartment packed up and shipped to your new apartment. Once you get him settled and then get yourself settled, you can, ah, start law school."

"I…don't understand," I say slowly.

But I *do* understand. I understand all too well.

"There's no reason for you to wear yourself out with multiple trips back and forth across the country. Just consider this a, ah, paid vacation and a paid move. With gratitude for your year of exceptional work."

"I can pay for my own move. I've been saving for it. Why should you pay for me to move when I'm leaving your company and taking my career in another direction?"

"I *want* to do it for you," he says on an incredulous laugh. Maybe I'm crazy, but anyone hearing all this fervency would believe he's eager to do whatever he can to help smooth this transition for me. His consideration touches my heart. Until he utters his next sentence. "It's the least I can do to help you out after the way you've helped me."

Helped him.

The words linger as though they've been suspended in the air by invisible strings.

Is *that* what I've done? Is *that* the highest rank I've achieved with him this whole time?

Helper?

Me: I'm crazy in love with you, Griffin.

Griffin: You're a great helper, Bellamy.

I switch topics, probably because I'm too chickenshit to ask him those questions. Any answers he gives right now are pretty much guaranteed to wreck me.

"But we haven't hired my replacement yet," I say, latching on to the most logical reason why I can't quit yet. Griffin is nothing if not logical. And there's a tiny but proprietary part of me that doesn't want to turn over my well-oiled machine to some unknown replacement whose face I've never even seen. "The office needs—"

"The office will be fine."

"Well, that's all settled, then," I say, stung by the implication that my hard work and I are so easily replaced. "And what about *you*?"

Another one of those moments passes when he opens his mouth but can't quite get his words in sync. Another moment when my entire life seems to hang in the balance and my gut tells me to keep hanging in there with him while my head shouts for me to cut my losses and run.

"I'll be fine without you. I was fine before you showed up in my life. I'll be fine again," he says, slicing my heart neatly in two.

18

BELLAMY

I'LL BE *fine without you.*

He says it with zero inflection. Zero expression.

Zero regret.

This whole cut-and-dried routine is seriously starting to do a number on me. Ending things between us is one thing. Ending it with the same demeanor he'd use to reassure his server that he doesn't mind changing his dinner order—*Oh, you're out of the halibut? Just give me the salmon, then; I'll be fine without the halibut*—adds a whole new level of insult to injury.

"And what about *us*?" I hate the slight tremor in my voice. It makes me sound weaker and more vulnerable than I already feel. "Since you have everything all planned out and I'm sure you've given this whole situation a lot of thought. What happens to *us* if I leave now?"

He tries to speak, but the words seem stuck in his mouth. I'd love to convince myself that there's a part of him that hates what he's doing, but I'm not sure I could manage it.

"We've had a great time together," he says, his voice

sounding rusty until he pauses to clear his throat. "But we always knew this was going to be a summer thing. Fall is almost here. It's time for you to go start your new life. And for me to go back to my old life."

Okay. So there it is at last. The reason he's been acting so weird since he got back. I reel in silence for a beat or two, almost relieved to hear him say it. Until the pain finally hits in some sort of a delayed reaction, leaving me to absorb this information the way I'd absorb a jab between my ribs with an ice pick.

It hurts too hard. Cuts too deep.

I'll be okay. I'm a strong and capable woman who has successfully managed this man for the past year. I'll manage this, too. But first, I need to figure out whether this is the same kind of defense mechanism he loves to hit me with whenever I get too close or a genuine *thanks for the laughs* kiss-off. I need to know whether he'll be heartbroken when I'm gone or whether his new assistant will send me the standard end-of-the-affair bouquet of flowers to my new home out west.

"So…that's it?" I ask.

"That's it."

"And you can't even look at me?"

Evidently, he can't. His attention remains fixed on some indeterminate point just past my shoulders.

"Look." A tinge of frustration creeps into his voice. "I don't know what you want me to say here."

"Just tell me. Is there someone else? Is that it?"

I hate myself for asking. But I need to know.

He softens. Just a bit.

"No, Bellamy."

Miracle of miracles, he meets my gaze for a fleeting second, long enough for me to glimpse turbulence in his flashing eyes but not long enough for me to analyze whether it comes from irritation that he's not rid of me yet or genuine regret. Even so, I believe that there's no one else. Maybe I'm a bigger fool than I ever feared, but I do.

"You're sick of me?"

He takes a deep breath and looks directly at me. We stare at each other, the moment stretching into infinity. Honest to God, I feel things clicking into place between us. Connections being made.

Part of him wants to lie. Part of him wants to tell the truth. Which part will win?

"No," he admits quietly.

"You don't care about me?"

He opens his mouth but doesn't answer. Maybe he can't answer.

"I think we should talk about this," I say. "Work something out. Because I'm not ready for it to be over. Are you?"

"It doesn't matter what I'm ready for or not ready for. I'm not the relationship type. Never have been. Never will be. That's not going to change."

"You can change whatever you want to change. You can *try*. I'm willing to try the long-distance thing. Or to try to see if I can go to school here. Maybe transfer to NYU next semester."

This information seems to unsettle him. "You shouldn't have to shelve your dreams to accommodate me. I'm not worth it."

"Maybe *you're* my dream."

"Get real. You need someone who's the relationship type. Not someone who fumbles around with it."

"Maybe I need *you*," I say, frustration making me

loud. It just took a fair amount of courage for me to admit the strength of my feelings for him. I didn't expect to receive a *get real* in response.

"Maybe *I* don't want to see you hate me when I keep disappointing you," he says sharply. "Maybe *I* need to think straight for both of us."

"Maybe you don't," I say, bristling at the implication. "Maybe you need to mind your own fucking business and let me make my own decisions. Pretend I'm a grown woman who can handle herself. Give me that courtesy."

"Courtesy?" he says, looking startled. "It's not about *courtesy*—"

"You know what? You're right. It's about honesty. It should be, anyway. So why don't you be honest? Get to the bottom line. Which is that you don't care about me enough to even try to make this work."

"Bullshit." Anger flares in his eyes. I know it's twisted, but this show of emotion excites me. Makes me feel as though we're circling closer to something important. Maybe even a breakthrough. "I care enough about you to let you go off to a better life without me. Go be with your father. Go find a man who deserves you. I'm setting you free, little butterfly. I just opened your cage door. Have the good sense to fly away."

"Oh. Is *that* what you're doing?" I infuse my voice with a liberal dose of mockery, knowing it will infuriate him. "Let me run right down to the store and get a thank-you card for your efforts."

"That's exactly what you should do," he says, vivid patches of red appearing across his hard cheekbones. "And when you come to your senses, you'll thank your lucky stars that I did the right thing by you."

I nearly choke on all his noble condescension. Ironic

how I'm so eager to provoke his anger that I can't control my own.

"Maybe I don't consider it the right thing!" I shout, not caring how many of my neighbors I wake up with my ravings. "Maybe I don't feel like I'm in a cage! Maybe I don't want to fly away! Maybe I want to stay right where I am!"

"Why would you?" he roars. "Because of my charm and sparkling personality? The sex can't be *that* good, sweetheart."

"No," I say, my palms itching to smack that sneer off his face. "Because I accidentally fell in love with you when I wasn't looking! And, believe me, no one's more surprised about it than I am!"

We stare at each other, both equally stunned by what I just said. A ringing silence follows. Until he scoffs.

"There's not enough here for you to love, Bellamy."

"Oh my God," I cry, stricken by this hint of the low self-esteem buried beneath all that bravado and arrogance. "What are you so scared of?"

The suggestion of cowardice riles him up again.

"I'm not scared! I'm clear-eyed enough to know that love isn't a thing. I'm smart enough to know that people don't do what they say they're going to do, and they sure as shit don't change. Which means that I'll never be who you need me to be, and you may think you want to stick around, but you'll wind up leaving one day. I know you will."

"You're right about one thing," I say. "The man I need would at least *try* to work things out."

He winces, silently absorbing this the way he would a slap across the face.

"There. See?" Crooked smile. No sign of humor anywhere. "Now you're getting smart."

I stand there like an idiot for a second or two, stunned by his unmistakable bitterness and grim satisfaction. It's like he's happy that I've agreed with him. *Happy*. I wonder what unseen wounds have driven a strong and proud man like this to such a low point. It's like he's been cursed to this miserable existence and doesn't understand that things could be different if only he'd meet me halfway.

And then it hits me. I knew he carried scars from his childhood. I just never dreamed I'd be able to draw a straight line from his mother walking out to this painful moment between us.

"Here's the thing," I say, forcing myself to keep it calm. "We've got some rough spots. But I think you and I are the best things that ever happened to each other."

He blinks and hastily turns away.

"I'm not walking away without a fight, Griffin. You mean more to me than my pride. So I'm telling you that I'm willing to try the long-distance thing. Or to consider transferring to NYU law for the spring semester. All you need to do is crack your heart open a little bit more and let me in. And maybe recognize the fact that your mother's memory is pulling the strings here —"

His head whips back around. He's furious.

"What?"

"Because you want to strike first and push me away before I push you away the way *she* pushed you away," I say, standing my ground.

I know I've hit his emotional nail on the head when he transforms right in front of me, turning into a sneering gargoyle version of the man I love. This sudden change is a bit scary, to be honest, and I resist the urge to back up a step. I feel as though I've finally met the real enemy only to remember that I left my sword in the car.

"All *you* need to do is crack your eyes open and realize that I don't have a heart to work with, Bellamy," he yells, his voice booming off the walls. "You're not going to fix me. I don't need your lectures or your psychology bullshit to tell me what's wrong with me. I live with it every fucking day. And don't you throw my mother in my face."

"I'm not throwing her in your face!" Rising panic makes me shrill. It's not that I think he'd physically hurt me. He won't. I'd stake my life on it. It's that this opponent is so much more fearsome than I ever imagined, and I feel like we're battling over Griffin's soul. "I'm asking you not to trash this relationship because you're too paralyzed to fight some ghost from your past!"

He makes an aborted sound, like a choked bellow. I get the feeling that he's losing his epic battle to keep all *that*—whatever *that* is—locked inside. His fists clench. His eyes flash. His entire body seems to strain against all this turmoil. And I fully understand, for the very first time, why I can't get close to him. He hasn't got a brick wall guarding his heart. He's got something a million times more effective. He's got *that*.

"What's not clicking here, Bellamy? Why are you making me rub your face in it? Try to listen this time: I was fine before you walked into my life and I'll be fine when you walk out of it! I don't need you! I don't need anyone!"

I watch him, riveted by his bravado and intransigence. Something about it reminds me of a little boy arguing that he doesn't need a bath. Completely illogical, but that's his story and he's sticking to it.

"I don't believe you," I say, staring him down. I don't know where this absolute certainty comes from. Only that it's as much a part of me as my brown eyes and hair. "Not for a second. Lie to yourself if it makes you feel better. You can't lie to me."

My relentless calm makes a sharp contrast to all his bottled agitation. His breath sounds harsh and his cheeks are flushed. He shows all the veiled fear of a man trying not to lose his ass while changing a flat tire on the interstate with cars zooming by at seventy miles per hour.

"Be as stubborn as you want," he says. "But facts are facts."

Stalemated, we face off in a brittle silence.

"Look," I finally say. "If you're not going to miss me when I'm gone, just tell me. I can live with that. But don't throw me away for no good reason. Because I seriously doubt anyone else will ever be as good for you as I am. And we both know you're going to be miserable when I'm gone."

He scoffs. But I notice he's not looking me in the eye again.

"Yeah. Okay. Anything else?"

"Yeah," I say, fed up with this chest-thumping performance theater. "You might want to practice shutting up a little bit more. Because you're going to come to your senses and want me back. You'll be looking for a way back onto the playing field. And the more you run off at the mouth now, the harder it'll be. So get your shit together, Griffin. Get. Your. Shit. Together."

19

GRIFFIN

"WHAT AM I DOING HERE?" I ask my brothers late one afternoon a week later, as soon as I walk into the library in the Hamptons estate, where they told me to meet them for reasons that remain unclear.

"Hello to you, too," Damon says, brows shooting up as he turns away from the drink cart with a bourbon for Ryker and a dirty martini for himself. "Drink?"

"What?" I say, beginning to feel slippage in the reins holding back my temper as I watch him pass Ryker his drink. Admittedly, my mood hasn't exactly been sweet for the last several days, but dropping everything at the office to race out to the Hamptons with no warning doesn't help matters. "A drink? Why the hell would I want a drink? I want to know what's going on. I get an urgent text saying you need me out here ASAP, then neither one of you answer your phones to tell me what's going on. Someone's dead, for all I know. Maybe the house slid off the bluff and floated out to sea. Now here I am, and I discover you two clowns sitting here having drinks like everything's peachy? If I'd wanted a drink, I could've stayed in Manhattan and had a drink *there*. What gives?"

"I told you this was a bad idea," Ryker says, then takes a sip.

"Yeah, I don't give a fuck," Damon says, setting his glass on the coffee table and returning to the drink cart. "I'm making you a gin and tonic, Griff. You're either going to drink it or wear it. Your choice. Now sit your ass down."

The reins slip another couple of inches. "I'm not—"

"Sit. Your. Ass. Down."

Funny thing about Damon: as the oldest brother and the one who looks the most like our father, he occasionally taps into a voice of authority that demands attention. Not that Ryker and I are scared of him. I wouldn't go that far, although he did beat my butt one memorable time when we were kids. Something to do with his broken model of the *Starship Enterprise*, if I recall correctly. No, we're not scared of him. We just wouldn't want to test him too hard when he gets like this.

So I sit down on a chair catty-corner to the sofa, shut up and check my watch. I don't do any of it with anything approaching good humor. "You've got thirty seconds."

"I'll take as long as I want," Damon says, splashing my drink together and handing it to me before sitting on the sofa with Ryker. Then he raises his glass. "To brotherly love."

"Fuck you," I mutter as we all clink. "What's up?"

"Well, Griff, you're causing a lot of problems at the office," Damon says, crossing his legs and brushing lint off his pants. "We called this little meeting today to get to the bottom of it."

"The fuck—?" I say, glancing at Ryker for confirmation.

He nods.

"First of all, no, I'm not," I say. "Second, why couldn't we have discussed these alleged problems back at the office?"

"We wanted neutral territory," Ryker says. "Otherwise, we couldn't guarantee your safety."

"What?"

"There's no good way to tell you this, Griff, but people want you dead," Damon says. "They're sick of your surly attitude and your rudeness. They're sick of your lack of gratitude. They're sick of your policy on khakis. No one wants to work with you. Everyone's started calling you the MF"ing Beast. It's bad."

I feel a slight squirm around my guilty conscience, but not enough to care. Since Bellamy left, I can't say I care about much of anything. And that includes eating, sleeping, working and behaving like a civilized human being. I'd hoped that my mood might lift in a few days or weeks, but that hasn't been the case. If anything, my mood has gone from bad to worse. It's the emotional equivalent of hot elephant shit, a rotting whale carcass and a ton of moldy Limburger cheese. Not that I care about pulling out of it or not inflicting myself on the public. Because, again, I don't care about anything these days.

That's not true. I care about this gin and tonic and getting to the bottom of the glass so I can move on to the next one.

"And this is my problem…why?" I ask.

"Because you're going to wake up one morning soon with your head on a pike," Ryker tells me.

I shrug tiredly, taking a healthy sip of my drink. The idea has some appeal. At least then I wouldn't have to keep seeing Bellamy's absent face every second of every interminable day.

"This can go one of three ways," Damon says. "Option one: we let the staff take care of you for us. I'll just tell security in the lobby not to stop them the next time they show up at the office with torches and pitchforks."

I snort.

"Option two," Damon continues. "We fire you to stop a human relations crisis from turning into a public relations crisis."

"It *could* work, except you can't fire me because I own a third of the company," I tell Damon, propping my feet on the ottoman.

"That's what *I* said," Ryker says.

"Well, that only leaves option three," Damon says, nailing me with a dire look. "You tell us what the issue is, and we try to figure out a solution."

I don't like the sound of that. For one thing, it should be obvious to anyone with half a functioning brain that Bellamy's absence from my personal and professional lives will take some getting used to. Plus, I don't intend to discuss the current depths of my despair with anyone, especially these two clowns.

"Look," I say. "Things have been a little dicey this week because I don't have an executive assistant. I'd hoped to start training one by now, but the agency keeps sending over underqualified candidates. The guy they sent over on Tuesday didn't even make it until lunchtime."

Ryker glances over at Damon and frowns. "Is that

the guy they found having a panic attack in the men's room after Griff showed him the ropes and told him his expectations?"

"Nope," Damon says tightly. "That was Monday's guy."

"That's right," Ryker says, snapping his fingers as his expression clears.

"It wasn't a full-on panic attack," I say. "I think he was hiding. Obviously, he wasn't ready for a big-boy job. The agency will send someone new over next week and things will settle down."

"That's the point, jackass," Damon says with rising frustration. "The agency is now refusing to send anyone else over to work with you. And I'm pissed that I need to get down in the weeds with this petty executive assistant bullshit. I've got bigger fish to fry."

I shift uncomfortably, feeling a vague stab of guilt.

"We'll find another agency. I'll get someone hired and trained. Problem solved." I down another healthy portion of my drink. "Are we done?"

"Problem solved?" Ryker chokes back a laugh. "Did he actually just say that?"

"He did." Damon looks substantially less amused. "As if his real problem isn't Bellamy."

I flinch, the sound of her name a nasty zap to some unidentifiable but tender point deep inside my body. "There's nothing to solve. She's gone. That's that. Don't mention her again."

"Yeah, but why is she gone?" Ryker asks.

"Try to keep up," I say, glaring at him. "She's going to law school at Berkeley. And I *just* told you not to mention her again."

"They have law schools *here*," Damon says quietly.

There's something empathetic in his expression that borders on pity. I don't like it. I don't like it so much that I down the rest of my drink and get up to make myself a refill.

"Yeah, well, her father lives *there*." I add ice a little more forcefully than I need to, causing a couple of cubes to ricochet out of the glass and onto the floor. "Anything else? Since you two seem determined to continue this pointless conversation?"

"Yeah." Ryker again. "We have an office out there. Why don't you relocate?"

I pour too much tonic into the glass, causing it to fizz and overflow. Cursing, I look around for a towel, mop up the mess and toss the towel aside. Then I plant my hands on the cart and lean into it, staring out at the rose garden and trying to get my thoughts together.

Why don't I relocate?

Like I haven't thought of that and a million other unworkable scenarios to keep Bellamy in my life.

Why don't I move out there? Why don't I beg her to move back here? Why don't we split the difference and settle in Kansas City?

Why don't I throw myself at her feet and tell her I can't breathe without her?

"Yeah, that won't work," I tell them.

"Law school's only three years," Damon says without missing a beat. "You could do the long-distance thing. It's not like you don't have a jet to get back and forth."

My throat gets tighter all the sudden, probably because I feel a swell of rising emotion. What emotion? No fucking idea. But it feels hot. Hard. I press my lips together, determined not to open my mouth unless I have some control over what might come out.

"Don't badger him, Damon," Ryker says. "For all we know, Bellamy wanted a clean break. Is that what happened, Griff? She cut you loose?"

I try to answer him, but now my mouth doesn't seem to work. It feels like I'm cranking the handle to control someone else's body.

"Griff?" Ryker says. "Is that what happened?"

"Nope," I say.

"Because there's a lot of fish in the sea out west," Ryker says. "Maybe she wants to dip her toe in the waters."

I don't know why the suggestion causes a haze of bloodlust to settle over my vision. I keep telling myself—and her—that I want her to find the kind of guy she deserves. A fresh new guy with a heart where a heart should be. But the idea of Bellamy finding someone new out there makes me want to pick up this entire drink cart and smash it against the nearest wall.

And I know what my brothers are doing. They're trying to help me in their own clumsy way. I just don't plan to open the lid on my twisted thoughts for their input.

"What she"—Christ; I can't even force myself to say her name—"does or doesn't do is not my business."

"Surprised to hear you say that," Damon says. "She's good for you. We can almost tolerate you when she's around. We weren't wild about you dating a subordinate, but I was beginning to think you'd marry her."

His use of the M-word does something to me, jars something in my brain and makes that dark emotion surge to the top. So much for holding the reins to my temper. I turn to face my brothers, my mouth working fine again.

"*Marry her*? What you mean, *marry her*? Why would I do that? Were you not paying attention when Mom and Dad ruined each other when they split up? You think that taught any of us anything about how marriage works?"

"No, but I've got a pretty good idea how it doesn't work," Ryker says ruefully. "All the stuff they did? I'm not doing that."

"Yeah, well, *you* do whatever you want to do," I tell him. "I'm not planning to ruin Bellamy. She deserves someone better than me. And I sure don't plan on watching her walk out on me one day."

"What, like Mom walked out?" Damon says.

"Yeah, genius, exactly like that," I roar. "Why does this have to be said? You were there. You experienced the exact same things I did. I still have nightmares about being alone in the stupid west wing—"

"Sorry about the nightmares, but Bellamy's not Mom," Ryker says. "Mom was never happy. Not that I recall, anyway."

"Damn straight. Bellamy seemed pretty happy to me before she left," Damon adds. "And she's already spent a year with you. Good, bad and ugly. And let's face it— you've got a lot of ugly. Seems like she knew what she was getting into. And she still got into it anyway." He shrugs. "Call me crazy, but I thought that was love."

"First of all, love isn't a thing," I say, furious. "Second, do you think Mom and Dad never thought they *loved* each other? Look how *they* turned out. Hating each other's guts. Mom walking out. Bitter custody battle."

"Maybe," Ryker says, shrugging. "But they fought the good fight. They tried to make it work. Which is more than we can say for you, if you just let Bellamy walk out of your life without trying to keep her around. If *that's* what you did, she does deserve someone better than you, doesn't she?"

I want to give him a heartfelt *fuck you*, but I can't quite work up the outrage. Not in the face of logic like that.

Bellamy told me that she's in love with me. She told me that she's willing to try the long-distance thing or to transfer to NYU next semester. And what did I do? Did I take her up on either of those wonderful offers? Did I collapse in gratitude?

Or did I duck inside my shell and play dead like a terrified turtle?

Hell, it was worse than that.

I told her I'd be fine. *Fine.* What a joke. *I* am a joke.

"Why would she want me?" I ask my brothers, dead serious even though I feel a sudden swell of hope. "A woman like that? She could have anyone."

"That's none of your business," Damon tells me. "She just does. Why don't you let her? You know she's the only thing that ever made you a tolerable human being."

I wince. "Because I know what it did to me when Mom walked out. I saw what it did to Dad. I'm not doing that again."

Ryker barks out a laugh. "You want some ironclad guarantee that your life is going to be smooth sailing? Fuck you. No one gets a guarantee. You go hide in the corner if you want to, big man. I'll be on the playing field."

Swear to God, something chimes in my brain.

You'll be looking for a way back onto the playing field. So get your shit together, Griffin.

I blink at my brothers, stunned back into my right mind.

"Looks like he's starting to get it," Ryker tells Damon, not bothering to hide his amusement at my expense.

"Yeah, but I'm glad we got involved," Damon says grimly. "With *this* fool? He'll screw things up every chance he gets if we don't help him."

I manage a weak laugh as my mind shifts to the problem of getting Bellamy back after the way I shot myself in the foot by letting her go without a fight.

I can't be mad at Damon's assessment. He's not wrong.

But I'm going to fix this or die trying.

20

BELLAMY

MY PHONE PINGS early that evening, just as I pull into a parking space and kill the engine.

I've got a text.

From *Griffin*.

We've only exchanged a couple of texts about my dad's successful surgery and Jeremy's treat habits in the week that I've been gone, so I try to keep my expectations low even though my pulse rate sprints into the red zone. He's not going to suddenly beg me to come back, no matter how much I wish he would.

It's been a long day and my nerves are already edgy, but I brace myself and look.

Need quick input on trying to find your replacement. Thoughts? Pls & thxs

I snort with disbelief and resist the urge to throw the phone out the window. The taste of bitterness floods my mouth.

I. Am. Such. A. Fool.

Griffin doesn't want to talk to me. Never that. He wants my help on his search for my replacement.

Much as I'd like to hit delete and possibly block his number, professionalism and curiosity get the better of me. I click on the attached document and check it out.

Currently seeking a highly qualified and motivated individual to fill an immediate vacancy. This position requires a minimum of one year's experience in the field and promises upward mobility, excellent benefits, profit sharing and golden handcuffs. Stringent noncompete and nondisclosure clauses are nonnegotiable.

I lower the phone into my lap, outraged. *Upward mobility? Profit-sharing? I* never got any of that! Is this a joke?

Skills in diplomacy, communications, negotiations and problem-solving considered essential. Special qualities such as strength, kindness, intelligence, humor and patience are considered a plus, as are beauty and sexiness.

Wait, what?

My heart stops, then starts again, beating out a frantic rhythm more appropriate for a hummingbird's wings than a healthy human. I clap my free hand over my mouth to stifle a semi-hysterical laugh, then keep reading as fast as I can.

The position includes late nights, travel, a potential relocation to the West Coast and, ultimately, an iron-clad lifelong contract.

"Oh my God," I whisper, laughing and sobbing now. "Oh my *God*."

Feisty individuals with zero tolerance for bullshit will be given priority. Only qualified applicants need apply. The position promises to be challenging but infinitely rewarding. All serious offers will be considered.

Now a complete mess, I hastily fish a tissue and compact out of my bag and reconstruct my face as best I can. Then I grab my phone again and call Griffin.

"Hey," he says after about half a ring.

"Hey," I say shakily, struggling to keep my head above the adrenaline and anticipation. God, even my hands are shaking. "I'm here for my job interview."

I can almost feel his wheels spinning during the long pause that follows.

"*Here*? Where? I'm in the Hamptons. My brothers dragged me out here to stage an intervention."

"I know," I say, and hang up.

By the time I get out of my car and walk up the cobbled driveway, I hear hurried footsteps on the other side of the massive front door. Then it swings open and there he is looking freshly showered and delicious in his T-shirt, knit shorts and wet hair.

Our gazes click into place and stay locked on each other as I slowly walk inside the foyer and he shuts the door behind me. It's like we're both searching for something and won't stop until we find it. He looks a little bit thinner. I notice that right away. His cheekbones seem sharper, and there are dark smudges under his eyes that weren't there before. His entire body seems strung with tension as he skims me from head to toe, noting my floaty white dress and strappy sandals. Words crowd the air between us, waiting to be said as we try to get the choreography right for this delicate dance between us.

His expression? Unreadable.

He clears his throat and takes a deep breath.

"Hi."

"Hi," I say. It's such a thrill to be back in the same room with him that I work hard not to melt with delight. But now is not the time. We have genuine issues we need to address.

"What're you doing here?" he asks quietly.

I hesitate, my cheeks burning. "I was in the neighborhood?"

He dimples but doesn't hit me with the full smile. Probably a good thing. In my current lightheaded condition, I'd probably keel over in a dead faint if he did.

"Ah," he says. "I thought you were going to say you wanted your dog back."

"My *dog*. I knew I was forgetting something."

More dimples, creating a responsive swoop deep in my belly.

"Actually, your brothers reached out to me," I tell him. "They sent the jet to bring me back. They seem to think I'm the only one who can handle you."

He makes a wry face. "Evil snitches. They staged an intervention earlier, matter of fact."

"They did seem pretty worried about you."

"Hmm."

A beat or two passes, during which it occurs to me that his expression isn't quite so impenetrable now. The steady warmth emanating from his blue eyes gives me courage.

"So…? What did I miss?" I ask him.

He chokes off a laugh. "I just had the worst fucking week of my life."

I try to look only mildly interested in this information. "Yeah? How's that?"

"I barely eat. Can't sleep. Hate everything in sight. I blame you."

"*Me?*"

"For walking out on me."

"Walking—?" I can't contain my outrage. "You sent me away!"

"Semantics. We both knew I didn't mean it."

"*I* knew. So is this you getting yourself back onto the playing field?"

"We'll get to that." He reaches out. "Come with me."

Bemused, I take his hand and follow him toward the staircase. But the renewed physical connection sends a shock wave between us, making me shudder. His hand is big. Warm. Strong. So achingly familiar and reassuring that it stops my heart.

Luckily, he's not immune. He pauses, cradling my hand in both of his as he raises it to his mouth for a lingering kiss in my palm. I feel the heat of his breath. Note the dark intent in his sidelong glance as he leads me up the staircase.

"Griffin…" I say helplessly.

I know we haven't worked anything out yet, but I need more. *More.*

"Shh," he says, squeezing my hand. "Wait. I need to show you something."

I do my best to swallow my impatience, at least until he turns left instead of right at the top of the staircase. Curiosity gets the best of me.

"Hang on. We're going to the west wing?"

He nods, heading to a set of double doors that lead to a suite of rooms. He reaches for one of the knobs, hesitates, squares his shoulders and reaches again. By the time he throws the door open and waves me inside, I'm ready to whoop and shout with triumph on his behalf because I know how tough this is for him.

But I keep quiet, determined to move at his pace.

"This was my mother's room," he says.

"I see that." It's quite the elegant sanctuary. Massive bed. Golden wallpaper. Silk drapes and matching upholstery that look as though they're the work of whoever decorated Versailles. There's even a fainting couch. French doors lead to a balcony that overlooks the sparkling ocean and a sun that hasn't begun to set yet.

The overall effect?

A moment out of time. Sadness. Nostalgia.

He sits on the bench at the foot of the bed, where he rests his elbows on his knees and makes prayer hands in front of his mouth. His gaze slides out of focus.

"My parents. My mother. They did a lot of damage."

"Those were *her* selfish choices," I say vehemently. "*Her* bad choices. She threw away her family. It had nothing to do with *you*."

"I know that."

"Do you?"

There's a pause.

"I'm working on it," he says ruefully, lowering his hands and staring down at them as he rubs them together. "To start with, I'm taking over this wing. Redecorating. The whole works. It doesn't need to be a shrine, and it'll help me make new memories. Be done with that chapter of my life. Hopefully, anyway."

"Wow. That sounds like a great start."

"There's more. I'm going to find a shrink to help me work on it. It's not the coolest thing I ever did. Admitting that I have mommy problems at the age of thirty-two. But I need to do it."

"Yeah? Why's that?" I ask, my pulse rate speeding up.

"Because it's the only thing standing between me and my dream life."

The silky note in his tone catches my attention, as does the way the heavy fringe of his lashes intensifies the vivid blue of his eyes when he looks up at me again.

"Your dream life?" My voice turns husky. "What does that look like?"

"Who knows?" he says, staring me in the face. "The only thing I know for sure is that you're in it."

My breath catches.

"I'm in your dream life?"

"You're in the middle of it, Bellamy. You know you are."

"I'm not sure I know anything," I say shakily.

"I propose that you transfer to NYU next semester. That'll give you time to help your dad get back on his feet, wrap up his business and come with you. We need a new head groundskeeper around here to make sure our roses stay alive."

My father? He wants to include my *father*?

The sudden surge of joy inside me makes it hard to talk. I'm too busy battling happy tears.

"I'm not sure my ears are hearing right."

"Come closer. I'm happy to tell you again."

That's the cue I've been waiting for. I can't get to him fast enough, fueled by euphoria and excitement. He surges to his feet, opening his arms wide, and I hop. The upshot? We come together like lovers during the proposal scene in some cheesy reality TV show, swaying together in each other's arms with my legs in a death grip around his waist.

"I don't know what I thought I was doing," he says in an urgent whisper, cupping the back of my head to bring me closer. He presses his nose to my hair and breathes me in, a shudder working its way through his body. "I'm terrible at living without you. You're all I think about."

"So why send me away?"

"Rank stupidity and cowardice. Why'd you come back?"

I pull back so I can see him and cup his face between my hands. In this overwhelming moment? I can't love him hard enough.

"I never listen to you when I can help it."

"Fair enough," he says, laughing as he swings me around and lowers me to the chaise lounge before going to work on his clothes. He sweeps his shirt off first, revealing all that sun-kissed golden skin and sinewy muscle. I'm sure I've never seen anything as mouth-watering as the sight of the ladder rungs he's got running through his abdomen without an ounce of fat on him. I'm thoroughly enjoying the view up top when he bends at the waist to get rid of his knit shorts, distracting me with his taut ass and the muscles flexing across his back. When he straightens, I see that he's fully erect already, that big dick straining for me.

"You better get started on your clothes," he says, his grin crooked when he sees the way I'm looking at him. "Unless you want me to ruin another dress."

"This won't take me long."

I hastily get up on my knees and unwrap my belt, letting the dress fall open and slither off my shoulders. My bra goes next, freeing my breasts with a gentle bounce that does not go unnoticed by him. I'd planned to kick off my little sandals, but he doesn't give me the chance before swooping in and rearranging me so I'm flat on my back.

"I'm not sure your mother would approve of us using her room like this," I say as he stretches out on top of me, levering on his elbows and getting into position.

His grin turns wry as I eagerly spread my legs for him. I'm already creamy between the thighs, with spirals of desire making my inner muscles clench. Any foreplay now would be as useless as augmenting the Sahara Desert with bags of sand from the local Home Depot.

"This is *our* room now," he says, taking his dick and running it through my juices, just to make sure I'm completely insane by the time he's done with me. "And I can't think of a better way to get her out of here."

There's time for a quick laugh, but then he lets out a serrated breath as he stares down at me. Suddenly the mood shifts between us, and this is no time for fun and games. I can tell it by the way his jaw tightens and all the intensity zeros in on me.

He curses.

"You're so beautiful, Bellamy. I lose half my brain cells every time I look at you."

Before I can respond—not that I know what to say when he looks at me like that—he thrusts hard, burying himself to the hilt inside me. My cry is sharp and helpless as I arch beneath him and scrape my nails up his back. Much as I want this to last forever, he stretches me too tight. Every minute movement of his hips hits every secret nerve ending that I possess.

Honestly, I never have a chance.

Especially when he starts talking.

"Do you know how much I missed you?" he says between endless kisses. "Huh? Do you have any idea?"

"I missed you too."

"You had me moping around the house. Every day. Even the dog was sick of my ass."

I can't stifle a triumphant laugh. I don't even bother trying. "Good. Serves you right. Maybe you'll think twice before you get any additional bright ideas."

"Don't worry," he says with a snort. "I've learned my lesson. I'm never letting you go again."

"Make sure you don't."

He kisses me again, his sudden tenderness taking me by surprise. He strokes my temples and cheeks. Trails his long fingers down my torso and takes his time about circling back to my breasts. Massages my thighs and encourages me to hold him tighter.

His thrusts slow down but keep their power, unerringly hitting my sweet spot and spiking my pleasure higher than it's ever gone before. He's not happy until I'm breathless with it. Until I tremble and moan with it. Until our bodies are slick with sweat as his belly rubs across mine.

I stare up at him, mesmerized by that brilliant blue and the way he now seems lit from the inside.

"I could die like this," I tell him, my voice barely audible. I'm not aware of crying until I feel a tear trickle down my temple, and he brushes it away with his thumb. "Exactly like this."

"Funny. 'Cause I would die without you."

I start to smile, but ecstasy chooses that moment to consume me from the inside out. It begins in rippling waves that mushroom to spasms that make my hips jack-knife as I shout nonsense. His laugh sounds victorious as he picks up his pace. I draw my legs in and smack his ass, and that's all it takes.

He stiffens and comes with a deep-throated rumble of triumph that makes me feel like the luckiest woman in the world. I hold him tighter, savoring the way his big body shudders and his shoulders heave as he tries to catch his breath. When it's over, we find ourselves facing each other with our heads resting on the same pillow, exactly like we did that first night together.

I notice everything about him. Those long lashes and heavy brows. The exact curve of his cupid's bow. The warm earthiness of his scent.

After a while, he musters a drowsy smile and traces my lower lip with his thumb.

"Glad you flew back, little butterfly."

I grin and lean in for a gentle kiss. "Glad you opened up and let me in a little."

"It's a relief. I feel a million pounds lighter. I had too much bottled inside." He hesitates, his eyes crinkling at the corners. "Especially the big thing."

"The big thing?" I raise a brow. "What, your mother, you mean?"

"No. I mean you."

"What about me?" I ask, bemused.

There's a pause.

His expression shifts, becoming luminous. He doesn't smile, but he doesn't need to. I've never seen a person look happier.

"I love you," he says quietly. "I'm crazy in love with you."

I take a beat or two to work that information past my heart, which is close to bursting, and let it sink in. I'm sure the dreaded beast will make a return appearance or several as we build our life together, and I'm fine with that. Especially when I've now met *this* wonderful and adoring man.

The one I suspected was trapped deep inside all along.

"I thought you told me love isn't a thing," I remind him.

"It is now," he says, gathering me closer again and tipping my chin up for his kiss. "It is now."

~

Thank you for reading *The Billionaire's Beauty*! I hope you loved Griffin and Bellamy's story as much as I do. And if you're wondering about Ryker's happily ever after, read *The Billionaire's Cinderella* now!

After meeting at Bemelman's, pastry chef Ella and Ryker go back to his apartment to eat her cake and watch *Jurassic Park*…

I still feel drawn to him.

Like, really drawn.

The same way a totaled car is drawn to one of those big electric magnets right before the poor car gets flattened into scrap metal.

He hits a button on the remote, dimming the lights. On screen, the handlers work on transferring the velociraptor into her new habitat. And Ryker retrieves his slice of cake and takes a bite with gusto.

"Whoa. This is insane," he says, eyeing me with wide eyes and a healthy new respect. "You know what you're doing with ganache and buttercream, sunshine. Kudos."

"Yeah?" Ridiculously pleased with myself, I pick up my own plate, mostly to give my fidgety hands something to do. "Glad you like it. I wasn't sure if I should add some—"

"Shh." He faces front again, the side of his mouth twitching with a repressed smile. "No talking during the movie."

"Funny," I say, and it seems like the most natural thing in the world to whack him in his taut abs with the back of my free hand.

From there, it seems like the most natural thing in the world for him to put his fork down, take possession of my hand and use it to reel me closer while never taking his eyes off the screen.

Well, what can I do? I'd already kicked off my heels when we arrived, so now I tuck my legs under me, arrange the throw across my lap and sit right next to him, in a spot where his bare right arm brushes against my bare left arm every time he takes a bite of cake.

I can't explain the effect these accidental touches have on my overheated skin. His body is big and hard beside mine, full of latent power and electrical charges. Nothing special happens between us, but it's like sitting next to a sleeping tiger. You never for one second forget yourself and mistake it for a housecat.

On screen, the scene switches to the lawyer wearing his white Panama suit in the jungle just as Ryker finishes his cake and sets his plate down.

As for me? I find myself mesmerized by his long lashes, straight nose and the strong lines of his profile. My attention dips to his tender mouth. To the dark smudge of ganache on the outer corner of his lower lip.

And I can't help myself.

I shift my position, until my bent knees lean against one of his muscular thighs. Then I reach out and gently run my fingers through his thick hair, giving his nape a little massage. You probably know me well enough by now to understand that I'm not big on making the first move. Or any move. But my boldness is rewarded when I hear his breath hiss and feel a shudder ripple through him as I withdraw my hand again.

I wait, not daring to move.

He takes his time about turning his head to face me. The movie throws his features into light and shadow, highlighting the sensual gleam in his eyes and the new tension in his jaw line. We stare at each other, his gaze skimming my lips and my hair before centering on my eyes and locking in.

"Time for my kiss?" he asks, his voice husky.

"I'm here to watch the movie. I just thought you should know you have some ganache on your mouth."

"Ah."

"You're a slob and a disgrace. I'm embarrassed on your behalf."

He rests his elbow on the back of the sofa behind my head then uses his thumb to trace swirling figure eights on the side of my neck, making me shiver.

"Take care of it for me, sunshine."

"I'll see what I can do," I say, leaning in.

I give the corner of his mouth a gentle lick, tasting man and chocolate. Ambrosia. And if I angle my head, licking my way past his lips and into the slick depths of his mouth, that's not the end of the world, is it?

He evidently doesn't think so. An approving rumble gathers in his throat as he shifts toward me, helping himself to handfuls of my hair on either side of my face as he deepens the kiss. He's got this way of being languid yet commanding, taking control and setting the easy pace with lush sweeps of his tongue. Our lips glide against each other, mapping and exploring. Figuring each other out. It doesn't last long. It doesn't take long. By the time he lets me up for air, my decision is made. There's no choice for me to make other than a graceful and eager surrender to the inevitable…

Read *The Billionaire's Cinderella* now!

SUBSCRIBE TO MY VIP LIST!

ALSO BY AVA RYAN

Fairy Tale Billionaires Series

The Billionaire's Princess

The Billionaire's Beauty

The Billionaire's Cinderella

Manhattan Billionaires

His Lost Love

His Forbidden Love

His Secret Love

To DH
XOXO

ACKNOWLEDGMENTS

Once again, special thanks to Nina Grinstead and the team at Grey's Promotions for helping me launch this baby and to Croco Designs for the lovely covers. Additional thanks to my writer friends for holding my hand and/or talking me down from ledges as needed. You know who you are. Hopefully, you still know how much I love you.

© Copyright 2020 by Ava Ryan
ALL RIGHTS RESERVED

This is a work of fiction. All characters in this book have no existence outside the imagination of the author and have no relation whatsoever to anyone, living or dead, bearing the same name or names. All incidents are pure invention from the author's imagination. All names, characters, places and incidents are products of the author's imagination or are used fictitiously. Any resemblance to actual events or locales or persons, living or dead, is entirely coincidental.

Except for use in any review, the reproduction or utilization of this work in whole or in part in any form by any electronic, mechanical or other means, now known or hereafter invented, including xerography, photocopying and recording, or in any information or retrieval system, is forbidden without the prior written permission of both publisher and Author copyright owner of this book.

Excerpt from *The Billionaire's Cinderella* © 2020 by Ava Ryan

ABOUT THE AUTHOR

Ava Ryan is an author of sexy contemporary romance. Her favorite things, in no special order, are animals, her family, cookies, people with great senses of humor and love stories. Currently in her writer's cave (ostensibly working hard on her next book while also checking Netflix every few hours to make sure she hasn't missed a new true crime documentary show), she loves hearing from readers via her website or social media.

If you love billionaire alpha males, the feisty women who snag their hearts and books that end with a happily ever after, you've come to the right place.

Please make sure to Subscribe to Ava's VIP List to stay in the loop about her latest releases and upcoming books.

Finally, don't forget to follow her on Amazon and/or BookBub to learn about any special promotions on her books.